Megan Sparks

Megan Sparks

Roller Girls

Falling Hard

With special thanks to Alexandra Diaz

First published in 2013 by Curious Fox,
an imprint of Capstone Global Library Limited,
7 Pilgrim Street, London, EC4V 6LB
Registered company number: 6695582

www.curious-fox.com

Text © Hothouse Fiction Ltd 2013

Series created by Hothouse Fiction
www.hothousefiction.com

Cover designed by Jo Hinton-Malivoire, original concept by
www.spikyshooz.com
Illustrations by Allan Campbell

ISBN 978 1 78202 032 5

1 3 5 7 9 10 8 6 4 2

A CIP catalogue for this book is available from the British Library.

Typeset in Baskerville by Hothouse Fiction Ltd

Printed and bound by CPI Group (UK) Ltd, Croydon, CR0 4YY

MIX
Paper from
responsible sources
FSC® C020471
FSC
www.fsc.org

Thanks to the Santa Fe Disco Brawlers

Chapter One

A doorbell ringing in the middle of the night usually meant bad news. Annie Turner squinted at the unfamiliar clock. 11.46. Something had to be wrong. There was something definitely wrong. She looked at the clock again. 11.46 A.M.

Then it all came back to her: the long and delayed flight from Heathrow to O'Hare, then the wrong turn her "I know the way" dad took that put them in Indiana. It wasn't until four in the morning that they had arrived at their real destination: Liberty Heights, Illinois. By that point, Annie couldn't do the maths to work out what time it was in London.

Ding-dong. The doorbell. Again. She tumbled out of bed and went in search of the front door.

Dad, with his brown hair sticking up to one side, met her in the hall. He looked as disorientated as she felt.

He pointed to the front door and opened it with a flourish. The brilliant sunlight burst into Granny and Grandpa's old house. Dad cowered and said in his Transylvanian vampire accent, "Argh, eet burns!"

Annie would have rolled her eyes at him if she wasn't squinting and holding her own hand out in front of her. It took several seconds to realize someone was standing outside. Two someones.

A petite woman with perfectly cropped blonde hair wearing a pressed light-blue shirt and white linen trousers. Next to her was a tall girl around Annie's age with wild brown ringlets that matched her skin. She sported a cool 1950s orange bowling shirt and real tattered jeans, not the kind bought that way. The two didn't look like they belonged in the same universe, let alone on the same doorstep. Only their hazel eyes were the same.

Oh, no. People. Annie should have remembered doorbells were usually rung by people and at least put on a dressing gown. Instead she stood there in her faded Winnie-the-Pooh nightie – the one that should have gone to the charity shop years ago but was so comfy she couldn't part with it.

The girl's wearing cool vintage clothes and I'm in Pooh. She must think I'm four instead of fourteen, Annie thought.

"Hi!" said the woman in a chipper voice. "I'm Marilyn Jones and this is my daughter Lexie. Welcome to the neighbourhood."

"Thanks. I'm David, and that's Annie." Dad introduced them, yawning.

Mrs Jones smiled, showing her perfect white teeth. "I work for the real estate agency and I have the keys of that diner down on Main Street you're renting."

Dad perked up immediately as he took the keys from her hand. "Old Al's. I'm turning it into a café."

"What a wonderful idea. Al's has been empty for so long – we were delighted to find a tenant." The woman thrust a basket into Annie's arms. "We brought these as a little welcome to Liberty Heights. They're blueberry muffins."

"Annie's favourite, huh, Beanie?" Dad said. Annie wanted to pull her Winnie-the-Pooh nightie over her head and disappear. Did Dad have to call her that in front of the new neighbours? Ever since she grew about a foot last year, and became too tall for gymnastics, Dad had been teasing her with a new nickname, String Bean.

"Thanks," Annie said to Mrs Jones. She'd deal with Dad later. "That's lovely."

Mrs Jones clapped her hands in glee. "Ooh, Lexie, did you hear her accent? *Lovely*. Isn't it the cutest?"

"Mo-om," Lexie said under her breath. She gave Annie an apologetic look, which Annie greatly appreciated. She liked Lexie already.

Mrs Jones turned to Dad. "But you don't seem to have much of a British accent."

"Wha-aat?" Dad looked at her in shock.

No, Dad. Please don't do your cockney accent. It's horrid, Annie pleaded silently.

But there went Dad with his ridiculous cockney accent.

"'Ave oi los' me accent, 'ave oi?" He sounded like Dick Van Dyke in *Mary Poppins*.

Annie covered her eyes with her hand, though the sun wasn't to blame this time.

Seeing that he'd embarrassed his daughter enough, Dad put his arm around her and returned to his normal voice. "I grew up here, in this very house." He nodded at the faded, floral wallpaper. "Still looks pretty much the same, in fact. I met Annie's mom in London when I was a student."

Mrs Jones peered over their shoulders. "Is she awake? I'd love to meet her."

Annie and her dad looked at each other. Right now Mum was probably at work at her law firm, even though it was Saturday. Without Annie and Dad living there any more, Mum might never come home from work. A knot tightened in Annie's stomach.

Dad squeezed Annie's shoulders and kissed the top of her head. "Philippa is staying in London."

Mrs Jones's eyes widened as she understood what Dad was saying. "Oh, I'm sorry. Well, if you need anything, *anything*, you just let us know, OK?"

Dad assured her they would as Lexie grabbed her mother by the elbow. "We should go. They need to unpack and stuff."

They all waved goodbye. Lexie mouthed, *Sorry*. Annie grinned in return. Definite friend potential.

Dad closed the door before wrapping Annie in a hug and kissing her forehead. Annie pressed her head into his chest.

"I'm glad you're here with me," Dad said.

"Me too," Annie said and squeezed him tighter. Dad had always been the one there for her while Mum worked as a lawyer; Annie couldn't imagine living without him. On the other hand, it was going to be weird living without Mum. It had been the hardest decision she'd ever had to make.

Dad must have known what she was thinking.

"We'll call your mom in a bit. Tell her we're here and all. But first," he dangled the keys Mrs Jones had brought, "let's check out Rosie Lee's."

"Yes!" Annie said. It had been her idea to call the café Rosie Lee's, which was cockney rhyming slang for tea. A reminder of home so far away. "But I want to shower and get dressed first."

Dad rolled his eyes and gave an exasperated sigh. "Girls. Always want to look their best."

Annie mimicked him. "Dads. Always in a hurry."

She ran a hand through her brown hair slowly and examined her fingernails for a few seconds while Dad tapped his foot impatiently. With a laugh, she dropped the act and sprinted to the shower. She was as eager to see the new café as he was.

For years Dad had impressed family and friends with his cooking and baking. He never followed a cookery book and yet he always seemed to know just how much to use and what flavours went together. When he'd seen on the internet that his old hangout, Al's, was up for rent, he'd decided it was finally time to put his kitchen skills to use.

"Growing up, Al's was the bomb," Dad said as they walked down to the café eating Mrs Jones's muffins. "Used to go there after basketball games for burgers and milkshakes. Even kissed a girl or two in the corner booth. No wait, that only happened to the other guys."

Annie listened to his stories as she checked out the small city. There was so much space! Every house they passed was detached and had a large front and back garden. Still, kids played on the quiet streets, moving out of the way when an occasional car drove along. Main Street, just a few blocks from her grandparents' house, with its rows of shops, had more traffic, but mostly just people looking for a place to park.

Outside the diner formerly known as Al's, Dad took a deep breath. "Wow, it's exactly how I remember."

Glass lined the whole front of the diner and a black and white canopy offered shade over the pavement in front of it. It looked cool and inviting. On nice days like today, Annie could imagine people sitting at tables enjoying a cream tea with scones and strawberry jam.

"Here, you do the honours." Dad handed Annie the keys. She drew out the moment, building the suspense, before finally turning the lock to the soon-to-be Rosie Lee's.

The sight inside was enough to make Annie wish they could run back to London. The photos they had seen online hadn't been taken recently. At least three different bug species scurried across the floor as Dad and Annie took tentative steps. Mouse droppings covered the greasy counters. The booths were gone (probably a good thing or they'd be mouse mansions) and the floor looked raw and naked. Dust, dirt, and grime covered everything.

The glass display case housed so much mould it looked like it had been taken over by a furry green monster.

Scenes from the play, *Little Shop of Horrors*, ran through Annie's head. If they were eaten alive by mould or insects, how long would it take for someone to discover their remains?

Dad ran a hand through his brown hair, making it stand straight up like it had this morning. "Let's not tell your mom how bad it is. I don't want to hear her say, 'I told you so.'"

That was exactly what Mum would say. When Mum had found out he wanted to open a café, she'd said food businesses were a waste of money. Annie didn't know if Dad was finally following his dreams or rebelling against Mum when he decided to rent his old hangout sight unseen. Either way, Annie couldn't bear to see her dad fail. He was a fabulous baker and if Mrs Jones's gooey and tasteless muffins were any indication of the rest of the town's cooking, he'd be an instant hit.

Annie took a deep breath. So what if Dad rushed into getting the place? It was still pretty cool. And cheap. They could renovate it and make it exactly what they wanted it to be. It was going to rock. Eventually.

"Well," Annie said. "Let's crack on, then." She turned on the 1980s boom box which had been left behind in the kitchen and found a station playing The Clash.

Dad grabbed a broom and was soon half sweeping, half singing into it as a microphone. When he'd lived in Liberty Heights, Dad not only played basketball, but was also in a garage band. The photos of Dad as a head-banging teen with long hair always made Annie laugh. Still, it was listening to his old CD collection that gave Annie her taste for classic rock, especially punk.

"I'm so glad you're here," Dad said between broom-guitar solos. "It'll be good for you to finally experience life in the States."

"I've visited Granny and Grandpa in Florida loads of times, remember?" Annie teased as she sprayed cleaner on the front windows.

"Trust me, Liberty Heights is nothing like Disney World and retirement communities. We don't go around with mouse ears here."

Annie squirted some spray in his direction. "I was five when I did that, and you bought a pair too."

"Rubbish," Dad said in a hoity-toity voice.

"So what is there to do in Liberty Heights? Besides clean and help out in this fab place?" Annie added quickly.

Dad looked at her mischievously. "I was hoping, now that you're too big for the uneven bars, you might enjoy basketball, like me. You're tall enough."

True. At five foot eleven (and a half), she was one of the tallest at her old school. But basketball? The last time she played netball during PE, the ball almost broke her nose. It was one thing to do a cartwheel on the balance beam, it was completely different to try catching a ball while running.

Dad set down the broom and leaned into it. "Well, how about cheerleading? It's kind of like gymnastics."

"Cheerleading might be fun. The routines they show on the

telly seem cool." Annie finished with the windows and threw the dirty paper towels in the bin. The difference clean windows made was astonishing. Looking through them, everything on the outside seemed to sparkle. On the inside … well, it still needed a lot of work.

Like attacking the green monster in the display case. Mum would have rung a professional team or thrown the whole case away but Dad wasn't a "house husband" for nothing. He sprayed it with bleach first ("So it won't bite back,") before pretending to wrestle it out of the display case. Once it was gone, lying dead in the bin, they disinfected the case again. No mercy.

After several hours, the place was beginning to shape up. Dad straightened his back with a few loud pops. Annie could feel a blister forming on her hands from all the scrubbing.

"Why don't you take a break, check out the downtown area if you like." Dad groaned as other parts of his body creaked. "And remember to look both ways. Cars drive on the right here."

Annie didn't need to be told twice. The sun was still shining and she couldn't wait to learn more about the place she'd be spending the next year.

"Don't work too hard." Annie kissed her dad on the cheek before racing back to the house. Her Rollerblades were easy to find; she had placed them in her hand luggage, so they wouldn't get lost. The clothes she had put on to clean in were dirty and sweaty so she changed to the first things she could find: a Sex Pistols T-shirt and jeans. She pulled her long brown hair into a ponytail and was ready to roll. When she got back, she'd unpack and start thinking about how to change the old-fashioned bedroom that had once been Aunt Julie's into something a bit cooler.

Taking a deep breath of the fresh air, Annie felt great. Jetlagged? No idea what that was. Sore hands from cleaning? Not any more. The sun beat down on her and there was a breeze coming from the river making it the perfect rollerblading temperature. Annie whizzed past Rosie Lee's and checked out the rest of the downtown. It didn't take too long. Post office, pizza place, chemist's, a few shops, the usual. Nothing like the hustle and bustle of London streets. She passed a small playground with swings and a slide – worlds away from Hyde Park where she and her friends had spent hours rollerblading.

Still, Dad had said Chicago was only a two hour drive away.

It'll be brilliant living here, she tried to convince herself.

She did crossovers as she turned a corner. A loose shaggy black dog darted right in front of her. Too close to stop, too sudden to think, Annie leaped over the knee-high mutt. She cleared him easily, but when she landed on the other side, the skates almost shot out from under her. Almost. Crouching low and waving her arms like a train conductor, she only just managed to keep her balance.

Phew, that was lucky. Annie straightened up and glanced around at the dog. Not so lucky. As soon as she turned, Annie crashed into a blonde girl who suddenly emerged from a shop. Annie, the girl, and her large frozen yogurt landed hard on the pavement.

Well, some of the frozen yogurt did. The rest covered the

girl's blazer and miniskirt.

"You freak!" the blonde girl screamed, looking down her front at the mess.

"Sorry, so sorry." Annie got back on her skates and offered the girl a hand. "Are you all right? I didn't see you. Or the dog. I'm really, really sorry."

"You should be." The girl refused Annie's hand and got up slowly on her own. "You could have killed me. And my clothes are totally ruined, thanks to you."

Surely a good wash would be all the blazer and skirt needed, but Annie still felt bad. She could definitely feel a bruise on her bum so the girl must have one too. "I really am so sorry."

Annie dug out a tissue from her pocket (she was pretty sure it was clean) and offered it to the girl. "Can I get you another frozen yogurt? I'm really sorry."

The girl swatted the tissue away with a look of disgust. "*Sorry*. Is that all you can say – *sorry*?" Every time the girl said "sorry" she said it in a very bad English accent. "If you're really *sorry*, why don't you go back where you came from?"

Annie didn't know what to say. She thought Americans were supposed to be friendly, even to the point of being overly so like Mrs Jones. Obviously this girl hadn't read the *American Stereotypes Handbook*.

Annie was saved from apologizing again by two brown-haired girls wearing similar outfits to the one now covered in yogurt.

"Oh my god, Kelsey. Are you OK? Can you believe her? Totally could have killed you." The two new girls gave Annie the dirtiest look before helping their friend into a gold Volvo four-by-four and screeching off.

Annie squatted down on her skates and cringed. First Winnie-the-Pooh, now Yogurt Girl. What a way to make a great first impression.

Something furry brushed up against her. Startled, Annie looked down to find the mutt mopping up the yogurt from the pavement. From the dog's neck hung a black lead and a skull-shaped tag with the name "Sid". She picked up the lead and looked around for Sid's owner. She didn't know what Dad would say if she brought Sid back to Granny and Grandpa's house, with its doilies and lace curtains and knick-knacks on every surface.

A tall black-haired skater boy about her age ollied and grinded the curb in front of her. Black-chequered Converse, black skinny jeans, and black chequered shirt over a black Ramones T-shirt. Good taste. And cute too.

He flipped the skateboard into his hands and blew his hair out from his bright blue eyes. "Sorry 'bout that. Sid Vicious doesn't know any manners yet."

Annie looked down at the human Sid Vicious on her shirt, then at the dog, and laughed – they were nothing alike. She handed the skater boy the lead with a grin. "I take it Sid's yours, then?"

The boy took the dog's lead and wrapped it around his hand. "Not that he knows it. Just got him yesterday from the pound. Only responds to food so far."

Sid jerked his head up, gave the air a quick sniff, and seemed to decide that the yogurt-flavoured pavement was still his best bet. Annie laughed. "What does he like best?"

"Sid here doesn't discriminate," the skater said with a grin. "This morning he stole my mom's toast and gulped it down like it was bacon."

Sid had his nose in the air again. There was no yogurt left on the pavement to hold his attention. Further down the street, a little boy was walking with his dad, eating a big bag of crisps and leaving a trail of crumbs in his wake. Sid sniffed his next snack. The skater boy threw his board down and jumped on it just as Sid took off. The poor guy was nearly swept off his skateboard. Nearly. Instead, the board did some kind of flip and his feet landed squarely back on it.

"Thanks for your help," he called over his shoulder. "You got some sweet moves. You should be a roller girl."

"Pardon?" Annie asked. But the dog Sid Vicious and the cute skater boy were gone in a second.

Annie sighed and skated around the slobbery pavement to head back home. Her bum was sore and her hands were sticky. Annie decided that her American-culture crash course was over for the day.

Chapter Two

First day of school. First day at an American high school. Annie just hoped the teen dramas on TV were fictitious. They didn't really put "kick me" signs on the new kids, did they? Pupils didn't really turn into vampires, hopefully. Dad wouldn't send her there if she'd be in any real danger, right?

Don't think about that.

She got out of bed and stretched with her arms in the air, before folding over and resting her hands by her feet. Ooh, nice. She sat with her legs stretched out on either side on the faded pink carpet and leaned over her left leg. Ahh, that felt good. She leaned over to the other side and let out a big breath. Amazing how some simple stretches could relax her. Maybe because they had been such a huge part of her life.

Stretching and gymnastics were my whole *life*, Annie thought. For ten years, she had trained five days a week and had her meets at the weekends. Annie had loved it, especially the thrill of competing. She could see if there were any training studios nearby – maybe they'd let her work out on the equipment just to keep in shape. Could be fun. Or could just be depressing knowing that she couldn't compete any more.

Maybe it was time for a change. To reinvent herself. New country, new interests, new life. Cheerleading, like Dad suggested. That could be fun. It'd be a change, if anything.

"Ann-nie," Dad called in a high-pitched American southern accent. "Y'all best git down here before this here breakfast goes and gets cold, y'hear?"

"Be there jus' as soon as I get mah duds on," she said in a cowboy accent that was probably just as bad as her dad's. Playing with accents had always been a favourite game of theirs. Good to know some things hadn't changed. Though, remembering the cockney accent he did in front of Lexie and her mum, maybe change was good.

Her open suitcases were still spread over the room; Annie and her dad had spent yesterday shopping for restaurant supplies, school supplies, and everyday-life supplies. What did people wear to school here? She had always worn a uniform, but according to Dad, she could wear anything. Within reason, of course.

The first things she found were her old leotards. She had given away the ones that were too small before she left London, but couldn't bring herself to get rid of all of them. It was always possible she'd find some use for them. Part of a fancy dress costume maybe, but definitely not for school. She tried on a T-shirt, skinny jeans, and her turquoise Converse – her "uniform" when she wasn't at school or the gymnasium – but it wasn't right. Not for the first day. Too scruffy.

"First impressions last forever," Mum always said.

She found the yellow summer dress Mum bought her before she left and put it on with some white ballet flats. Big improvement. For one thing, the dress showed off her long legs and if the sun kept shining, maybe her legs would soon be tanned, as well as long.

In the kitchen, Dad had prepared a full English fry-up: bacon, eggs, sausages, tomatoes, and fried bread. The smell reminded Annie of everything she'd left behind: Mum, London, home.

Dad waved his hands at the food. "Eat, eat. You're too skinny."

Annie picked up a triangle of fried bread and dipped the end into the egg yolk. She nibbled on the corner. "It's gorgeous, really. I just…"

Annie sighed, unable to eat much more with her stomach in knots. Dad kissed her on the top of her head.

"I know, Beanie. A lot has happened in a short amount of time and new schools are always scary. But it'll be fine. I'll take you to school. Go with you to the office. Just like I've done before on your other first days."

Except the last time Annie started a new school she was eleven.

It was time to do it on her own. "Thanks, but I think I'd rather go by myself."

Any other time Dad would have put on an accent and demanded whether he was not cool enough to be seen with his daughter. She loved that about him: he was funny and messed around a lot, but he always knew when she needed him to be serious.

"OK. You remember the way? We drove by it yesterday. And take your new cell, just in case you need to call."

Annie smiled. "Now you're sounding like Mum."

"Surely not!" he said in Mum's clipped tones.

Annie took a small bite of tomato and gathered her new bag, making sure she had her phone turned to silent in the front pocket.

At the door, Annie turned around. Her dad was watching her, a fork-speared sausage held in the air.

"I'll come to Rosie Lee's after school. And Dad, try not to burn the place down." She smiled and left before Dad could think of a comeback.

Outside, any confidence she had faked disappeared. Maybe she should have let Dad take her. Hold her hand as they walked into the high school.

No, she could do this. Just like that time they mixed up the music for her floor routine, playing the theme tune to *Chariots of Fire* instead of the White Stripes' "Seven Nation Army". She did her routine anyway and placed second. She could go to school alone, and survive.

Up ahead, Annie caught sight of a familiar head of wild brown ringlets. Lexie. The other day she seemed nice. Was she really, or was that just because her mum was there?

"Lexie," Annie called. Nothing. But there was a definite bob to Lexie's head which implied listening to music. Jogging to catch up, Annie tapped Lexie on the shoulder.

Lexie turned and broke into a huge smile. "Hey, good to see you again." She took the headphones out of her ears.

"Yes, likewise. I'm a bit nervous, though," Annie said.

Lexie scrunched up her nose. "School's not my favourite place either."

"Is that why you were playing 'Highway to Hell'?" Annie teased.

Lexie looked at her in surprise. "You like AC/DC?"

"I prefer more punk, but hard rock is good too."

Lexie nodded her approval. "We really should hang out. C'mon, I'll show you where to get your schedule."

Annie let out a breath she didn't know she had been holding. "Cheers. I love your clothes, by the way."

Today Lexie had on a denim jacket covered in cool badges like "Be yourself, everyone else is taken" (Oscar Wilde) and "eARTh" over a green lacy shirt, long hot-pink skirt, and tan cowgirl boots. Tied around the base of her wild hair was a purple scarf.

"Thanks, I get them at thrift stores. Mom hates it. Says the clothes are dirty and only poor people buy there. She wishes I could be a bit more preppy but I don't like looking like everyone else."

Annie nodded. The first time Mum saw her Sex Pistols T-shirt, she threatened to throw it in the bin. She smoothed out her new dress. "Do you think I look all right?"

"*I* think you look fine, but you should know, image is a huge thing at this school."

Annie didn't have time to ask what she meant. They were at school already.

A flashy red car zoomed right by them, turned the corner quickly, and screeched to a stop centimetres before crashing into the parked car in front of it. Its driver got out and locked the doors with the remote in his hands, making the car beep twice and its lights flash. Mum's car did that too, but her Peugeot had never contained anyone that made Annie gasp for air.

"Is he for real?"

Lexie rolled her eyes. "I know, right? Just because he can drive he thinks he's all hot."

What Annie meant was whether he really existed. The only time she'd seen a guy that good looking in the flesh was when she and her friends went to the Abercrombie & Fitch store in London where they have live models walking around. This guy didn't have to think he was hot, he *was* hot. Perfect blond hair fell across his forehead, making Annie long to brush it back. His light-blue shirt hung off broad shoulders, showing off his tanned, toned arms, and his jeans fit like they were custom-made for him.

Halfway to the school he took off his sunglasses. He was close enough for Annie to see his startlingly green eyes. Were they contact lenses? Surely that colour didn't occur in nature.

She watched him as he trotted up the steps and high-fived a group standing by the doors. *He's obviously very popular*, Annie thought. *Must have loads of girls chasing him.*

"C'mon, I'll take you to the office and show you to your first class." Lexie took her by the arm and led her away. Good thing too. Any more staring and she might start drooling.

She got her timetable and immediately showed it to Lexie. Back in England she would have been starting her GCSEs, studying subjects based on what career she wanted. Here it seemed they wanted her to know a little of everything.

Lexie's eyes widened. "Wow, you're in a lot of advanced classes."

Annie shrugged. She never got poor marks but was hardly top of her class either. "British school system, I guess. We start younger, I think. Are you in any of my classes?"

"Are you kidding? I'm not really into school as long as I pass. As soon as I'm done here, I'm off to New York for art."

Lexie pointed to Annie's class and waved before heading to her own. Annie went through the door as if it were going to bite. She knew not to sit in the front, but the back was crowded with a group of kids, including, Annie groaned inside, Yogurt Girl from the other day. Kelsey or something. She slipped into a middle-row desk and wished for invisibility.

The English teacher, Ms Schwartz, was fiftyish with hennaed hair in various shades of brown and red with a few whisks of grey sticking straight out like television aerials. She wore a hemp blouse and canvas trousers. Annie had never had such a

Bohemian-looking teacher.

"OK, class, I have two very exciting announcements. First we're starting Dickens's *A Tale of Two Cities*." There was a loud moan from the class. Annie wasn't worried; she'd read it last year. Hopefully she remembered it well enough not to have to read it again.

"And," Ms Schwarz continued, "we have our very own Londoner with us this year, Annie Turner. Can you come up here, dear?"

Now Annie *was* worried. She heard whispers from the back of the room that sounded a bit like "yogurt" and "freak". *Why, oh why, did teachers always insist on humiliating their pupils?* She slid out of her chair and shuffled up to the front. With a deep breath, she looked up and faced the class.

As she expected, Kelsey was giving her the evil eye, but what she hadn't expected was to see the gorgeous guy from the car park. Unlike Kelsey, he seemed eager to hear what she had to say.

"Why don't you tell us a bit about London? Last time I was there was just after Charles and Di got married. It must have changed so much since then," Ms Schwartz said.

Yes, Annie was sure it had. Except she hadn't even been born that decade so she couldn't say what had changed. "What would you like to know?"

Immediately questions started flying and Ms Schwarz, enjoying the excitement, didn't do anything to gain control.

Annie soon realized that what she wanted to say was quite different from what she actually said.

"Do you know the Queen?"

Yes, we have tea every fortnight. "No, but my mum's met the Prime Minister."

"Is it true the Scottish don't wear anything under their kilts?"

Aye, so best stay clear if there's a breeze. "I've never checked."

"Do you drink tea like all the time?"

Course not. We stop to sleep. "We do like tea, yes, but we drink other stuff too, like fizzy drinks and squash."

The sound the class made was a combination between "huh" and "eww". Obviously "squash" didn't translate well. She just hoped the American meaning wasn't rude.

Annie was about to explain that squash was a concentrated fruit drink when Kelsey spoke up. There seemed to be no avoiding her. Or getting her in a better mood.

"Is granny chic, like, a really popular look in London?" Kelsey said, looking at Annie's new dress with a smirk. A few other girls sniggered.

Before Annie could retort with a clever comeback (one she hadn't thought up yet), Ms Schwarz spoke up.

"OK, that's enough. Kelsey, let's not be rude. Annie, you can sit down, thanks."

Annie didn't have to be told twice and rushed to her seat both embarrassed and upset. She liked her dress and she wasn't going to stop liking it because someone insulted it. Especially someone like Kelsey.

When the bell rang, Annie gathered her things, wondering if she would be able to find her next class on her own. She noticed someone alongside her and blinked a couple of times. The gorgeous guy was there. Right next to her.

"Hey," he said.

Talking to her.

"Hey," Annie repeated, looking up into his green eyes. That seemed like a good response. She certainly didn't know what else to say.

"I'm Tyler. You're from London? That's so cool. What class do you have next?"

Surprised and more than a bit confused, Annie looked at her timetable while her stomach performed back flips. Sure she was tall and some people said she looked kind of like a younger Kate Middleton, but gorgeous guys like Tyler didn't normally talk to her. Still, she wasn't going to question it. "American History. Room 183."

"That's on my way. I'll take you there."

"Thank you." Was this really happening? Not only was this guy talking to her, he wanted to *keep* talking to her. She didn't know what it meant, but it had to be good.

"Do you like soccer?" His smile was so dreamy Annie wished she could have a poster of him up on her bedroom wall. A floor-to-ceiling one.

Wait, he's stopped smiling. Oh, right. He's waiting for a response. What did he say?

"I don't play soccer, but I do like watching it," she said slowly, hoping that covered what he asked. It seemed to work; his smile returned.

"What do you think of Manchester United?"

Annie hesitated, though this time not because she was lost in dreamland. Football rivalries ran long and deep. Opposing fans often got into arguments – sometimes even fights. What she said about Man U could determine whether Tyler kept talking to her or ran away. "I saw them play against Chelsea once. My dad took me."

Tyler stopped to look at her in awe. "No way! I've seen Chicago Fire play a couple times but that's nothing compared to what you have across the pond. I catch your games on TV sometimes, or online."

Annie smiled, glad Dad was more of a football than rugby fan. "It is nice to watch them live if you have the chance."

"Totally." He stopped by a classroom and jerked his head at the door. "This is you. See you around."

"Cheers – I mean thanks." She smiled back and stared at him as he walked away. She was really starting to like American high school.

"Out of my way." Kelsey knocked into her as she walked past. Or maybe not.

Chapter Three

Annie's knowledge of American History was limited to what she'd picked up from Dad and what Hollywood portrayed. Somehow she didn't consider either source reliable. They were studying the American War of Independence, or the Revolutionary War as they called it over here. Annie knew almost nothing about it. There were other, much bigger wars to study in British history.

"Hope you Brits aren't still sore about losing," the teacher teased as he passed by Annie's desk. Annie kept her head down and focused on taking notes.

Between Algebra and French, Annie realized she really needed a wee. She asked a couple of girls standing by their lockers. "Excuse me, could you tell me where the loo is, please?"

They looked at her as if she was from Mars. "The what?"

Annie blushed. "Sorry, the ladies' room."

A light seemed to turn on in their heads. One of the girls pointed. "Oh, sure. Just around the corner on the left." But before Annie had even started in that direction, the girl turned to her friend. "Don't you love her accent? It's so cute."

If only people would stop making such a fuss over her and the way she talked. At her old school, she had never stood out. She kind of liked it that way. Maybe Lexie could get her a badge that said, "I've got an English accent. Get over it."

After French, Annie consulted her timetable again. Lunch. Brilliant. Half the day done and she was starving. Next time Dad made her a fry-up, she was not leaving it untouched.

"Where do I queue up?" Annie asked a heavy girl with a green chequered shirt, biker boots, and short spiked blondish-brownish hair.

"I'm sorry, I don't understand," the girl said, looking puzzled. She seemed sincere but Annie was tired of being different and decided to work it out herself instead of asking again. It wasn't too hard. There was a queue for food, one for drinks, and a third to pay.

Pay. Oh dear.

Dad had given her some money for lunch. The notes were easy enough to sort out with their numbers even though they were all the same size and colour. But the coins were a nightmare. Annie felt like she was dealing with play money when she looked at them. She couldn't understand why the five-cent coins were larger than the ten-cent ones. It made no sense.

Deciding where to sit was another question, though she wasn't stupid enough to ask this time. She quickly noticed Kelsey at a centre table with her ladies-in-waiting and some guys, including Tyler. Not that Annie was bold enough to have sat next to him anyway.

At another table sat a red-haired girl Annie recognized from English class – the one who'd asked the kilt question. She was with some cool but tough-looking girls who were showing off arm and hip bruises. Annie remembered how she used to compare injuries with her gymnastic friends. These girls must play the same sport.

With a sigh, she sat by herself at a far table. It was less intimidating than asking if she could sit with people she didn't know. Well, at least no one was noticing her now.

"You bought lunch? That's brave."

Annie looked up from her cheese toastie. Lexie, thank goodness. "I shouldn't have bothered. It tastes like cardboard and I don't think it's really cheese."

Lexie plunked down her tray next to her. "It's not. Legally they have to call it 'cheese product' now. But whatever you do, stay away from the Sloppy Joes."

"That bad?"

"If they're anything like the ones in middle school, they're edible, but they'll leave you in the bathroom for the rest of the day."

Annie cringed and set down her sandwich. "What are you eating?"

Lexie held up a polystyrene cup and grinned. "Ramen noodles. I'm practising for when I'm a starving artist in New York."

"Is that your dream, then? To be an artist, I mean, not a starving person."

"Yup."

"Are you any good?"

In response, Lexie pulled out a thick sketchbook from her bag. She seemed to have a little of everything in the book, from caricatures with big heads to cornfields rustling in the wind and abstracts with geometric shapes. She even had a family portrait that captured their personalities: Lexie wild and individual, Mrs Jones preppy and perfect, and Mr Jones, who Annie hadn't met yet – he seemed serious and intellectual judging by his glasses and tweed jacket. All of the sketches were really good.

"I like the comic strips the best," Annie said.

"Me too. They're the most fun. I'll probably join the manga club."

Annie took another tentative nibble of her sandwich. "Your abstracts remind me of things I've seen at the Tate Modern."

"You've been to the Tate?"

"Yeah, and most of the other museums. School trips, you know," Annie added quickly so it didn't sound like she was boasting.

Lexie stabbed her noodles and broth with a fork. "I don't know how you left London. I'd give anything to go there. I mean Chicago is OK, the Art Institute is fabulous, but it's kind of far and there's nothing much besides cornfields between here and there."

Annie was kept from saying anything by a loud burst of static and then the principal's voice over the sound system. "Hello, students. I just wanted to remind you that this Friday is our first pep rally."

Lexie covered her ears as the cafeteria exploded in a cheer. This must happen regularly because the principal waited a few seconds before continuing. "And if you like what you see there, please note that cheerleading try-outs will begin after class on Friday. Thank you and keep those brains in gear."

"Ha-ha." Lexie rolled her eyes. "Is it over?"

A pep rally. Just the sound of it was so American. Annie had no idea what to expect. "I'll probably try out for the cheerleading."

"Why?" Lexie made it sound like Annie had said she wanted to grow a second head.

Annie shrugged. "Dad suggested it and I thought it'd be fun. I used to be quite good at gymnastics before I got too tall."

"I'm sure you'll be great at it. I just didn't think you were the cheerleading type, that's all," Lexie defended herself.

"What's the cheerleading type?"

Lexie ran a hand through her wild hair. "You're right, I shouldn't be prejudiced. I'll tell you what – if you make the squad, I'll come to a game, just to cheer *you* on. Cool?"

Annie nodded. Lexie hadn't answered her question but she wasn't going to push it. It meant more that Lexie was willing to support her even if she didn't like it. That was a sign of a true friend.

The rest of the day passed in a blur with Biology, PE, and Technology, and a few more exclamations about her "cute" accent. When the final bell rang, Annie grabbed her books and raced over to Rosie Lee's. She found Dad in the kitchen area by the sink wearing old dungarees and a wrench in his hand.

"I'm warning you," he said, shaking his wrench menacingly. "If you don't stop this instant, I'm going to rip you apart piece by piece."

"Talking to the mice, are you?" Annie asked.

Dad jumped and dropped the wrench on his foot. "Holy cow, Annie, you scared the bejesus out of me. What're you doing here?"

Annie dropped her bag and sat on the counter. "Let me have a think. I work for MI6 and I'm here to spy on you?" she said sarcastically. "It's after three, Dad. School's over for the day."

Dad looked at his watch and then held it up to his ear as if he didn't believe her. "Drat, the thing's stopped working again. Well, how was school? Learn anything?"

Only that American boys are massively hot (at least one in particular) and the cafeteria food is close to deadly. "There are some differences, but it's still school. What about you?"

Dad let out a melodramatic sigh. "Fine, except this faucet won't listen to me and keeps dripping."

Annie turned to the tap. Now that he mentioned it, it was making a steady *drip-drip* rhythm. "Maybe you should call a plumber."

Dad crouched down and attacked the pipe under the sink. "Nonsense, I know what I'm doing."

Annie didn't say anything. She didn't have time. Dad had barely touched the pipe with his wrench when the pipe burst. Water sprayed everywhere as Dad tried to stop it with his hands. "Turn it off, turn it off!"

Annie looked around, her arms held up to block the stream. "Where?"

"The valve. Out back. Hurry."

Annie raced out of the back door. *Valve, valve, where are you,* she thought, searching wildly. Inside she could hear her dad swearing at the water, pipe, and everything in between. She finally found it, turned it one way, heard Dad scream louder, and turned it the other way.

Back in the café Dad sat in a pool of water with his legs out in front of him like a rag doll. His hair was plastered to his face and water dripped down his cheeks.

Annie turned away. She bit her lip and covered her mouth. Her shoulders started to shake. She couldn't help it. She let out the biggest belly laugh she had in a long time. Dad slapped the floor and pouted like a baby, but soon he too was laughing. It took several minutes for them to calm down. Finally, Annie helped pull Dad to his feet and got out the mop.

"I think that's a sign to call it quits for the day," Dad said as he emptied the mop bucket.

"Good, cos I'm starving." Annie placed a hand on her slim belly. "Tomorrow, I'm bringing my own lunch, even if it is babyish."

"Food, now you're talking. What do you say we get pizza? Real Chicago style. Trust me, nothing else compares."

"What's so great about it?" Annie asked.

"For one thing, deep dish. For another, the sauce is on top."

"Really? Why?"

Dad thought about that for a bit. "I don't know the historic reason but as a cook, I'd say it keeps the crust from getting soggy."

"Any kind of pizza sounds great right now."

Dad ordered the pizza and they picked it up on the way home. For the first time that day, people were noticing Dad in his wet dungarees instead of Annie. Dad, of course, was all for the attention. After the second person gave him a funny look, he started strutting like the rappers on television.

"Da-aad," Annie said under her breath.

"If people are going to look, might as well give them something to look at." He jerked his head and gave a downward hand gesture to the old lady who stopped with her shopping to stare at him. "'Sup?"

Annie grabbed his arm and moved him away quickly. She wouldn't put it past the lady to take a swing at him with her shopping bag. He let up only when they were a street away from the house and there was no one around to appreciate his soggy rapper look.

At home, they polished off the pizza, by far the best Annie had ever had, and she headed up to her room to get started on her homework. She pulled out her new mobile and looked at it.

No calls.

It's the middle of the night in London, Annie reminded herself. But she wished Mum had remembered it had been her first day at school and had thought to ring. She finished her homework quickly – the teachers were obviously still easing them in after the long summer holiday. She turned on the computer hopefully. Maybe there was word from Georgie or Mel. Yes, but more importantly, there was an email from Mum.

Dear Annie,

I miss you already. The flat feels so empty without you. I just got in from the office, I've taken on a big case so it looks like I'll be doing even longer hours than usual. I hope your first day at school went well and that you found the lessons interesting. I ran into Nicola's mum yesterday and she sends their regards. I know that you must miss your friends but I'm sure you'll make new ones in no time. Let's plan to Skype later this week; it feels like such a long time since you left.

Love Mum xxx
PS Remember to keep your room tidy!

That was nice. Good to know she hadn't completely forgotten. But still, a call would have been better. Things had been tense between them since Annie had decided to live with Dad instead of her. Hopefully, Mum wouldn't hold it against her forever.

Annie flopped on her bed, pushing the clothes she rejected

this morning onto the floor. A second later she was up again. Remembering Mum's PS, she picked the clothes up, folded them, and put them in drawers. Funny how Mum could still manage to nag, even with an ocean between them!

Chapter Four

"Liberty Heights, are you ready to meet this year's very own Staaaaaags?" The announcer roared during Friday's pep rally in the gymnasium. The whole school cheered in response.

Well, not the whole school. Lexie doodled in her sketchbook while Annie clapped politely. She'd survived a week at school, and it wasn't too bad; the classes were fine and she knew her way around now. She was still "that English girl with the cute accent" but there were worse things they could call her. Like "punk", which is what Kelsey muttered every time they crossed paths.

"Put your hands together for the marching band and the cheeeeeerleaderrrrrrrrs!"

The band struck up a catchy tune while three cheerleaders ran out and did a round off into two back handsprings.

One of the brunettes bent her leg.

The other didn't stick the landing.

But that blonde one was impressive.

Annie's brain clocked their gymnastics abilities without even realizing it. She and Lexie were at the top of the tiered seats – the "bleachers" as Lexie had called them. From that distance, the cheerleaders' faces were a blur – but she was too preoccupied with their form anyway. After ten years of gymnastics, old habits died hard.

"We're the Stags?" Annie asked, unable to take her eyes off the cheerleaders as the rest of the squad joined the first three in a blur of silver and blue uniforms.

Lexie grunted as she drew caricatures of the cheerleaders with devilish antlers.

The marching band was building up. Something was going to happen. Like a wave on either side, the girl cheerleaders fell into back bends as two of the guys walked on their hands down the middle. In a chain reaction, the girls kicked over and landed back on their feet. A second later the handstand guys flipped back to their feet. The crowd went wild. Annie could feel the adrenaline as if they were clapping for her.

"Why don't you like pep rallies? This is fun." Annie clapped and cheered with the rest of the audience. "We don't have anything like this back home. We Brits are much too reserved."

Lexie sighed. "It's so egocentric. All this for sports, while the arts get cut all the time. And they don't have as many pep rallies for the girls' teams, even though last year the girls' basketball team won the regional championship."

Three different cheerleaders stood side by side, two climbed on top of them, and one more got on top to make a six-person pyramid.

"Who do we love?" they all shouted.

The audience screamed, "The Stags!"

The girl at the top of the pyramid fell back into the waiting arms of the guy cheerleaders, the two girls in the middle somersaulted forward and landed square on their feet, while the three at the bottom slid into splits.

Wicked! Annie imagined herself in the pyramid. She'd probably be on the bottom because of her height. She could do great splits, but she'd rather be in the air. More thrilling.

As the band launched into the school's song, Annie turned her attention back to Lexie. "It is unfair female athletes don't get the same attention. It's like that back home, too. I think gymnastics is one of the few sports where it's the opposite."

"It's just plain sexist. Do you know what our girls' teams are called?" Lexie shaded in her caricatures.

"The Deers?"

"If only. No, they're the Staggettes."

Annie scrunched up her nose. "That is a bit naff."

"I don't know what 'naff' means but from the sound of it, I totally agree." Lexie turned a page in her book and began sketching the teachers with massive heads and dopey eyes.

"Thank you, cheerleaders and band members." The principal got on stage and the crowd quieted. "We have two games this weekend so let's hear it for both the football and the soccer teams!"

The teams came running in from opposite ends of the gymnasium. The players stood in front grinning while the crowd cheered for them. Annie leaned on the edge of her seat, squinting to get a better look at one of the soccer players. Was it him? Yes, she was sure of it. That gorgeous run-your-hand-through hair and fit body. No wonder he was so keen to talk about the Premier League. Standing among the other soccer players, wearing the captain's armband, was Tyler.

He waved at the crowd and flashed such a dazzling smile that Annie was glad she was sitting; she might have swooned had she been standing. As the noise died down, the principal addressed the crowd again. But Annie didn't hear a word he said. All her attention was on Tyler, who was now chatting and laughing with the cheerleaders.

Well, that settled it. She was definitely trying out for cheerleading.

After her classes finished, Annie raced to the locker room and quickly changed into a night-sky leotard and a pair of navy shorts. It had been a while since she'd worn a leotard, but it felt like a second skin to her. *Good thing I didn't give them all away*, Annie thought. She scraped her long hair into a ponytail and was ready.

There were about thirty girls and two guys in the gym that

now felt incredibly big without all of the pupils there. Everyone stood around looking at each other, not knowing what to do, and not saying anything. If the idea was to make them anxious, it was working.

The door at the far end of the gym burst open and out came the cheerleaders in an intimidating group. This morning Annie had thought their outfits were nice. Now the girls in their blue and silver sleeveless shirts and pleated skirts over blue shorts looked almost menacing.

Or maybe it was the fact that at the front of the pack, next to the coach, paraded Kelsey.

Of course. She was the one who had done the perfect round-off and back handsprings, and the two brown-haired girls next to her were her wannabes, also known as Bent Leg and Didn't Stick the Landing. Annie had been sitting too high up in the bleachers to get a clear view of her face. Seeing the expression on it now, Annie began to wonder if cheerleading was a good idea after all.

"As you know, I'm Kelsey, the captain," Kelsey spoke in a bossy voice that echoed across the whole gym. "We're going around with clipboards to get your details before we start."

Kelsey's eyes landed straight on Annie.

Oh please, let her go to someone else.

She didn't. She strutted right up to Annie and jutted out her hip. "This isn't roller derby, you know. Sure you're in the right place?"

Annie blinked. "Uh, yes?"

"Whatevs." Kelsey slapped the clipboard into Annie's chest.

"Fill this out, but try to use normal spelling."

Annie wished she could think of some clever comeback that would make Kelsey back off. Nothing. Nothing clever anyway. She was at least pleased she was able to put, under experience, that she trained at the West London Gymnastics Centre (not Center).

Once they had everyone's details, Bent Leg (whose real name was Ginger) and Didn't Stick the Landing (Lulu) led the group into warm ups: jumps where you switched hands to tap the outside then inside of your heel and then the inside and outside of the other heel. It felt like Irish dancing with a lot more arm movements. Annie knew there were other ways to get the heart rate up without looking so silly and wondered if it was deliberate.

Then they did some stretches, focusing on warming up their back, hips, shoulders, and abs. For thirty seconds they had to hold a straight plank as if they were about to do push ups. Easy-peasy. In gymnastics training they used to do one-arm planks. A couple of girls dropped to their knees, then quickly got back into the exercise when Kelsey glared their way.

Next they had to complete a circuit from one end of the gym to the other: three cartwheels on each side, straddle jumps, a backbend from standing, splits, and finally a sprint to the end of the wall.

Annie had no difficulties doing the circuit and felt fairly certain she did it well. The coach gave her the smallest nod but Kelsey looked like Annie was giving off a bad smell. Sigh. If Annie didn't make it on the squad she'd have a good idea why.

"Gather round," Kelsey said. "I'm going to teach you a dance routine. Try to keep up, 'cause really, a baby should be able to do it." Kelsey scowled at Annie as she said it.

The dance was to an awful pop song that was just as popular in the UK as it was here. *Argh, this tune will stay in my head all day.*

Kelsey showed them the dance first before breaking it down. It seemed to involve quite a bit of hip thrusting and provocative gestures, or maybe that was just how Kelsey was doing it. When another girl joined her, the dance didn't seem quite so suggestive. Annie decided to go with the other girl's style.

The steps weren't any more challenging than a floor routine and Annie caught on quickly, though some of the other girls found it hard. One of the girls who struggled with the fitness part turned the wrong way, burst into tears at the sight of everyone glaring at her, and ran out of the gym. Annie watched her leave, waiting for someone from the squad to go and comfort her. No one did and Annie wondered if she should. It was like survival of the fittest and at least Annie knew she was fit.

Just as Annie was beginning to imagine herself at the top of the pyramid, the hopefuls were taught the basic cheer.

"I want to see huge smiles on everyone and powerful projection from the diaphragm," the coach said. "Remember cheerleading is ninety-nine per cent attitude and presentation. If you're not perky and peppy, you're not doing your job."

This was the hardest part in the whole try-out: all the "rah-rah" stuff when Annie only wanted to go "argh-argh". Even her gymnastics trainer in London had tried to get her to smile more: "Think grace and serenity. No one wants to see the effort behind it." Grace and serenity might not be the look the cheerleading team was going for, but Annie was sure they didn't want to see the effort either. Even smiling felt fake.

That was something she'd have to get used to, being more outgoing, more American. More like Dad.

"OK, that's it for today." The coach clapped her hands. "Use the stuff you learned to come up with a routine for Monday for the actual try-out. Don't forget your enthusiasm and those smiles."

Annie forced her mouth into a smile and hoped it didn't look too much like she was in the dentist's chair.

Chapter Five

"Hey, I scored some tickets for Saturday's game. Chicago versus Chelsea. Wanna go?"

Tyler ran his hand through that irresistible hair and locked his intense green eyes on Annie's.

Annie smiled at Tyler. She had on her silver leotard under the blue and silver cheerleading miniskirt. She looked good and she knew Tyler thought it too. "Of course. But I'm supporting Chelsea."

Tyler took a step closer, his eyes never leaving hers. "I don't care, as long as I get to spend time with you."

"Good." Annie reached out a hand to pull him closer. She'd never made a move on a guy before, but this was no ordinary guy. Tyler was gorgeous and … fading. No, wait, stop!

He didn't. He kept fading until he was gone and Annie woke to find herself in bed, the sound of bowls clashing and the whirr of an electric mixer coming from the kitchen.

It was Saturday, so Annie didn't have school and she could stay in bed forever. Except the smells coming from the kitchen were too tantalizing to ignore.

Who needed sleep anyway? She knew she wouldn't be able to get back to the dream about Tyler.

Coffee was brewing, waffles were cooking, raspberries were on the table, and Dad was hand-whipping the cream. It was almost as good as any dream. Getting asked out by Tyler would have been better, though.

"Am I the best dad, or what?" He tasted a bit of the cream with his finger. "Dang, that's good."

Dad already had a waffle on a plate which he placed in front of Annie. He stood there, waiting, as she loaded it with raspberries and cream.

She took a tentative bite, just to make him sweat. The waffle was perfectly crisp while the cream was fresh and the late-season raspberries from the local farmer were deliciously sweet. She couldn't lie; she wasn't as good at bluffing as Dad.

"All right, I admit it. You are, undoubtedly, the best dad ever. These are fantastic."

Dad leaped into the air and punched it. "I knew it."

"But before it goes to your head, you'd better check the next waffle." Annie pointed to the iron that was smoking. Dad rushed to take out his waffle, which was only slightly browner than ideal.

"So, what's the plan for today?" Annie asked once they'd finished their breakfast.

"I was hoping we could hang out with my other daughter."

"Rosie Lee?"

Dad rolled his eyes exasperatedly. "She said something about a makeover. I don't know. I have trouble understanding what girls want these days."

Annie laughed. "I'll get my painting clothes on."

Even before the "makeover", Rosie Lee's was really starting to come along. It no longer resembled a place you'd likely get a side order of food poisoning. The former rodent tenants had been evicted and the display case mould hadn't returned to get its revenge.

They spent the morning and most of the afternoon painting the inside of the café an off-white that worked as a blank slate. The difference it made was huge: now it was fresh and clean and…

"Naked," Dad said.

Annie turned around to get the full view. "Yeah, it does feel like it's missing personality."

Dad nodded. "I'm not sure what theme I want. Something cool and hip. Maybe some black and white photographs of famous London landmarks? Or maybe a local artist wants to hang their work? Just as long as it doesn't look like my mom runs the café."

"Really? I thought some lace curtains would be nice at the windows and quaint tables with flowers and teapots covered in tea cosies…" Annie bit her lip and stared out of the window. It was the only way she wouldn't laugh.

Dad shook a finger at her. "No! Stop! This is a doily-free zone. I have to keep some manliness."

He backed up to check out the bigger picture.

"Dad, watch—" Annie started.

Too late. He stepped in the paint tray and tripped over the bucket as he tried to straighten himself. Globs of paint poured out even though he straightened up the bucket immediately. His trainer was covered and left footprints all over the floor. "That wasn't the look I was going for."

Annie laughed. "At least it has personality now. And it's definitely not Granny's style."

Dad made a face before he started laughing too. Together they cleaned it up, but there was still a stain embedded on the floor, and Dad's shoe remained covered in paint. He scratched his head. "Now I have to figure out what to do with the floor."

A buzzing sound made them both jump and it took Annie a second to realize it was her phone.

Want to hang out?

Annie looked up. Dad was scratching his head as he stared at the paint stain on the floor. "Are we done here, Dad? Lexie just texted."

"Sure, go have fun. Leave me here all alone to clean up the mess." Dad threw his head back dramatically with his hand against his forehead.

"Do you really mind?"

"Course not." Dad dropped the act and gave her a hug. "I'm glad you're making friends. See you later."

She had never been to Lexie's house though she knew which one it was. A light-blue colonial with perfect white trimming, it made all the other houses look scruffy by comparison. Even the front garden was perfect. Not a single blade of grass seemed to be out of place. Lexie had said her mother took out a ruler to measure the grass's length. Seeing it up close, Annie thought it might actually be true.

Lexie opened the door for her and the inside was no different: perfectly arranged as if it were staged for an interior decorating magazine shoot. It was so immaculate it was hard to believe anybody actually lived in the house.

Lexie's room, on the other hand, was completely lived in. Messy and artsy, it was exactly how Annie imagined it would look. One wall had a mural of a made-up world with pointy-eared people flying across the green sky and aliens fishing in the orange river. The other walls were covered with other artwork, posters of New York, and a mood board of the looks Lexie was going for that autumn. The desk and dresser were covered in clothes and accessories Annie was sure came from charity shops.

Annie helped herself to the clothes pile and put on a lime green tutu over her shorts and a pair of purple and pink legwarmers. She stood with her legs wide and crossed her arms in front of the mirror.

"You lookin' at me?" she said in a loud tough-guy voice to the mirror. The mirror was too scared to talk back, making Annie laugh at herself.

Lexie looked up from her fedora. "Wow, you actually look cool. Like a roller girl."

"Right." Annie turned from the mirror, her arms still crossed. "Everyone keeps mentioning that and I have no idea what it is. Is it some American slang?"

Lexie laughed. "Better. Roller derby is a sport played on roller skates."

"Like hockey on wheels?" Annie asked.

"No ball or puck or whatever. Here, I'll show you. Easier than explaining." •

Lexie fired up her computer and pulled up some videos. They watched one with a pack of girls skating around in an oval and two other girls trying to break through them. One of the girls found a hole, snuck through, and the crowd went wild as she skated away on one leg.

"That looks wicked!" Annie exclaimed as they watched a video of one girl ducking through an opposing player's legs to score points.

"I know, right?" Lexie grinned. "And it's so much cooler live. Hey, check it. The Illinoisies are playing tonight in Prospect Park. That's not too far. Maybe we can get Mom to drive us."

"Think she will?" Annie asked.

"Sure, but let's make it sound like it's your idea."

They rushed down the stairs and found Mrs Jones in the back

garden tending to an immaculate flower bed of red, blue, yellow, and pink flowers. Lexie quickly told her about the roller derby and said that Annie really, really, wanted to go. She asked her if she could take them.

Mrs Jones set down her shovel. Even the silver blade gleamed under the rich dirt. "I suppose so. There's a house in Prospect Park I've been meaning to check up on."

"Yes!" Lexie spun in a circle like an excited dog.

"We'll go after dinner. Come down in about twenty minutes."

"Thanks," said Annie.

They dashed back up to Lexie's room. Right away, Lexie began flinging clothes in one direction and the other. "What to wear, what to wear?"

Lexie did have a point. Annie still had on her paint clothes and the tutu wasn't really an option, no matter what Lexie said.

"Bingo!" Lexie emerged with black-patterned tights and a pair of hot pants covered in gold sequins. She held them out in front of Annie. "Can you believe someone actually gave these away? They're a bit tight on me but should fit you just fine."

"What should I wear with them?" Just as Annie said that, a red vest top came flying in her direction, which she caught with one hand.

She pulled on the outfit Lexie picked for her and immediately felt like she was five and dressing up in her mum's clothes. Not that Mum ever had clothes like these in her wardrobe of smart business suits.

"I look like a tart," Annie said. She tugged at the hot pants, not that it helped. They were still insanely short. "I can't go out like this."

"Are you kidding? You have legs to the moon. You've got to show them off. How do I look?"

Annie turned to her. Cream fishnets, which contrasted beautifully against Lexie's brown skin, black micro-mini, and a pink off-the-shoulder shirt. On her ears were large hoop earrings.

"Like we're both tarts."

Lexie brushed that away. "C'mon. That's the fun part. Derbies are great places to let your alter-ego show."

Lexie's alter-ego was obviously part punk, part gypsy.

Annie relented. She was secretly impressed with her look. And even more impressed after Lexie applied extensive eye make-up. Well, it wasn't like she'd see anyone she knew.

Mrs Jones gasped when she saw how they looked. "Girls. You can't wear that in public. What about that cute corduroy skirt I bought you at the Gap?"

Lexie rolled her eyes. "Ma, that's so not my style."

Mrs Jones was about to argue when Mr Jones put a hand on her shoulder. "Marilyn, let it go. She's a teenager." Sounding like the anthropology professor that he was, he added, "Lexie's discovering her own identity. Adolescents in every culture go through this process."

"I suppose you're right," Mrs Jones sighed.

Mr Jones smiled when he responded. "Just this once."

He put an arm around his wife, which made her almost disappear into his chest. Mrs Jones purred contently before straightening up. "You're my snuggle-bun."

"And you're my precious jewel." He looked at Mrs Jones as if they were alone.

"Guys, please." Lexie covered her face as if she was going to be sick. "Stop before I have to report you."

Annie thought it was great, though it gave her a bit of a pull in her stomach.

Lexie's dad was tall and African-American, the complete opposite of his petite blonde wife. Still, they seemed to complement each other perfectly. Mum and Dad were opposites too, but even before they separated, Annie couldn't remember a time they got along as well as Lexie's parents. She hated that her parents had split up. It made her feel split up too. But at least they weren't fighting now.

Mrs Jones dropped them off at the university's ice rink with cautions of not talking to strangers and to call if they needed to be picked up early. Lexie rolled her eyes but promised they'd be safe before they ran into the building. Rock music was blasting through the sound system and it was filled with families, college students, and what Mum called alternative types: green hair, tattoos, piercings. Maybe it was a good thing Lexie had dressed her up, otherwise Annie would have stood out for looking too "normal".

They paid for their tickets and searched for a place to sit. The ice rink had been thawed, and three taped ovals, one inside the other, marked the boundaries. Folding chairs were set up on three sides of the track, but the only seats left were far at the back or the "suicide seats" on the floor.

"Is it safe?" Annie asked as they sat on the floor very close to the taped boundaries next to a sign that said "Crash Zone".

Lexie shrugged. "Kind of. They skate in the inner circle. If anyone comes your way, move – or you might end up with a roller girl in your lap!"

Annie felt someone staring at her and turned around to see the black-haired skater boy she met on her first day – the one with the dog Sid Vicious. He gave her a thumbs up as soon as their eyes met. She thought about heading over to say hi when the announcer started up.

"Goooooooood evening, ladies, gents, and all those in between. We have a great bout for you today. During the day, these ladies are moms, teachers, architects, herbalists, lawyers, you name it. But when they lace up those skates, they become the Corn Hustlers and our very own Illinoisieeeeeeeees!" The crowd let out a loud cheer. Unlike the pep rally, Lexie had no problem showing her enthusiasm as she stomped her feet on the rink floor. The announcer went on to introduce the women on each team. Most of their names were either sexy or vicious with puns intended like Viva La Diva or Psych O. Killya. The women showed off their moves, and muscles, as they skated around the track in tights, short shorts, stripy socks, and yes, one was wearing a tutu. They knew they were hot and tough, but it was all tongue-in-cheek.

Four women from each team huddled up at the front and started skating when the ref blew his whistle. A few seconds later, two women further behind sprinted towards the group.

"All right then, explain the rules to me," Annie said. Everything was happening so fast, it was hard to follow.

Lexie didn't look away from the women as she explained. "Basically, the two girls in the back with the stars on their helmets are the jammers. They're the ones who score. First they have to break through the pack – that's the rest of the girls. Then they skate fast around the rink to get behind the pack again and try to pass the members of the other team. Each opposing team member the jammer passes is worth one point. The other team is trying to block the jammer from scoring while helping their own jammer score points. They get penalties for pushing, elbowing, and things like that. If it's a major penalty, they get sent to the box."

Annie watched a few more rounds before asking her next question. "Why is that one girl, Bette Noir, flapping her arms at her hips?"

"She's the lead jammer, the one who broke free from the pack first. She can call off the jam whenever she likes. Usually to keep the other team from scoring or if she thinks she can't get more points. The lead jammer changes each jam, but Bette is the Illinoisies' star."

The bout was fast paced, full contact, and unlike any sport Annie had seen. Women got pushed, shoved, and knocked down all the time, but they'd get up and get right back in there. Sure they swore and called each other rude names, but as soon as the whistle blew, they were laughing and helping up members of the other team. And best of all, they seemed to be having a great time.

By half time, Annie was noticing holes in the pack where she would have squeezed through if she were a jammer. At one point, there was the most golden opportunity, if only the jammer, Poison Envy, had taken advantage of it. There was no one in front or behind one of her teammates who was bent low. The jammer could have easily vaulted over her teammate to score lots of points. At least if the jammer had been the imaginary Annie.

As the bout continued, Annie kept seeing herself in the jams. The other day when she ran into Kelsey was no fluke, she was a fairly good skater. But she'd never been in a position where other people were deliberately knocking into her.

It was a close contest, 72-69 to the Illinoisies. Waiting for Mrs Jones to come and get them, Annie noticed some leaflets on the merchandise table.

Fresh Meat Junior Roller Derby three-day workshop.
Girls 14–18. All skill levels. Get fit and have fun.

Mrs Jones honked. Annie hesitated for a minute, then grabbed a leaflet.

"C'mon, my mom hates to be kept waiting," Lexie said.

Annie folded the leaflet in half and slipped it under her vest top before running to the car. She was pretty sure Mrs Jones in a bad mood would be even scarier than the roller girls she'd just watched!

Chapter Six

Annie checked her bag to make sure her leotard and shorts were there. When she'd finished conjugating French verbs, she ran through her cheer in her mind, "Give me an S, give me a T, give me an A…" Cheerleading try-outs were happening after school, and Annie was having a hard time thinking about anything else.

It didn't help that Kelsey was obviously trying to psych her out. During lunch, she walked by with her two wannabes.

"I don't know why we're even having a try-out. We already know who we want. Obviously no one freakishly tall," Kelsey said loudly. Pretending that she'd just noticed Annie, her voice turned candyfloss sweet. "Oh, hi, Amy. I didn't see you there. Good luck today. You're going to need it."

Annie slouched into her seat while Lexie shouted, "Her

name's Annie, you dumbass."

Of course Kelsey knew her real name. Just like she knew Annie has been there listening to her. But was it true that they had already selected their new members?

"Am I really freakishly tall?" Annie asked the bacon sandwich she'd brought from home.

Lexie put an arm around her shoulders. Sitting side by side they felt like the same height. "You're not that tall, she was just trying to strike a nerve. She's just jealous of those supermodel legs of yours. You're so not a freak."

Annie sighed. "I guess. But maybe I shouldn't bother trying out."

Lexie shifted so she could stare right at Annie. "Look, you know I don't like cheerleaders. But you can't let someone like that stop you from doing what you want. That's what *she* wants. She only said it because she knows you've got a good shot."

Lexie did have a point. Of the kids who were there last Friday, Annie was definitely one of the top gymnasts. And her dancing wasn't half bad either. It was that perky, rah-rah, smile-until-your-lips-fell-off part that was her problem. "You're right. I'm not going to let her scare me off. I just wish she wouldn't make me feel so nervous."

"I'll tell you my secret." Lexie looked around the cafeteria like cartoon characters do when they're trying to be inconspicuous. "In my head I draw a moustache on her every time I see her. The result is actually pretty good."

Annie laughed. Thank goodness for Lexie.

* * *

The locker room was like a ghost town with no one speaking or even acknowledging each other. They were too focused on primping up in front of mirrors, curling or straightening their hair, and reapplying make-up. One girl was even stuffing what looked like chicken fillets into her sports bra. When Annie sat down on the bench to change, the girl next to her moved her make-up bag away like she was afraid Annie would use it.

"I'm not going to touch it," Annie said. Everyone stopped what they were doing and stared at her for a few seconds, then returned their attention to whatever they were doing. Except the girl next to Annie; she got up and sat somewhere else.

They filed out to the gymnasium and waited to be called forward. Annie hadn't expected to see so many people watching the try-outs; it seemed like half the school was there. She glanced around, wondering if there was anyone she recognized. Lexie had her manga club so Annie knew she wouldn't be there. But she didn't expect to find Tyler sitting with his friends on the second row.

Oh God. Breathe, Annie, breathe.

He caught her staring at him and jerked his chin up in greeting. Annie raised her hand a bit and turned away shyly. Crowds didn't usually make her nervous, but now that Annie knew that Tyler was there, her hands began to sweat.

"Listen up," the coach said in a voice that echoed throughout the gym. "You've got two minutes to show us what you've got in cheering, jumping, and dancing. I don't care if you do each element individually or one act that incorporates them all, just as long as you have a bit of all three in the two minutes. Quintana, you're first."

A girl with a high dark-brown ponytail and too much make-up came forward with a perky smile. Her cheer was loud enough for everyone *outside* the gym to hear and her dance moves were spot on. She didn't seem to have too much of a gymnastics background, but she could jump high and do cartwheels and backbends in good form.

The next one was a guy who thought he was a great breakdancer. Annie was sure head spinning was very hard, but the poor guy was so awful that it was more painful than impressive to watch.

"Turner," the coach called Annie forward.

Deep breath. Annie chose to do the cheer part first to get it over with quickly.

"Give me an S—"

"Louder," the coach yelled.

Annie tried to project more. Except her tongue just got muddled in her mouth. "Give me an S. Give me a, uh, T. Give me an S-T-A-J, I mean G, and S. What do you, uh, get? The Stags! Yay."

She pretended to wave pompoms in the air (*Why hadn't she grabbed some real ones?!*) and slid into a split. She ended it with a terrified, showing-all-her-teeth smile.

The crowd clapped politely but Annie's attention was on

Kelsey. Her face was set in a smug grin and she held out both her hands in the shape of a fat zero.

Annie's eyes narrowed and she shook her head slightly. *Sorry, mate. You're not winning that easily.*

Annie chose to modify a previous floor routine to show off her jumps and dance abilities. It was a high-energy number that displayed her flexibility, coordination, and ten years of gymnastics. Hands-free cartwheels, 360-degree straddle jumps, fancy footwork, and the sassy attitude she hadn't managed in the cheer. She ended it with a series of back handsprings into a back tuck, which she landed perfectly.

Take that!

The crowd went wild. Tyler was on his feet, clapping his hands above his head, and he gave her a heart-stopping smile.

Annie walked back to the bench feeling like her legs were made out of jelly. The rest of the hopefuls stared at her with mouths agape. Annie almost felt sorry for the next girl, though she wouldn't have done her routine any differently. Kelsey's smug smile had morphed into an ugly grimace and her stare was attempting to laser through Annie. Annie shrugged and wore a real smile for the rest of the try-out. Who cared what Kelsey thought? Annie had performed a great second part, and everyone, including the best-looking boy in school, knew it.

* * *

Annie was still feeling pleased with herself as she headed to Rosie Lee's after the try-outs. She just hoped her old floor routine was good enough to make up for the disastrous cheer. If only they'd let her get away with just doing the tumbling and dancing parts of cheerleading and leave the "rah-rah" rubbish to the ones who were good at it. And actually liked it.

She opened the door to the café to find Dad rushing around muttering, "Fire, fire!"

"What? Where?" Annie looked around in a panic and sniffed.

"No. Meant fire marshal. Must set appointment. Can't open." Dad ran around the kitchen looking up and down for something.

"What do you need?"

"Keys. Car keys."

Annie spotted the bunch of keys in the front pocket of his shirt and pointed. "Dad, there they are. It's OK. I'll go with you, help you sort it out."

Dad took the keys from his pocket and finally seemed to notice she was there. "No, there's nothing you can do, unless you can give me a brain transplant. I've got to get more organized if I ever want to get this place going. Thanks though."

Dad kissed the top of her head as he headed out.

Typical Dad; he could whip up the world's best crème brûlée but filling out paperwork was beyond him. He'd already taken the Illinois Food and Sanitation Course, and passed with flying colours, as well as setting up the business licensing, but she wasn't surprised there was still more to do. She just wished she could help him in some way. Do something that was sure to make Rosie

Lee's a great success. She stared at the naked off-white walls and the raw floor with the paint stain still on it, and they stared back at her.

That was it!

Annie grabbed her phone from the bag. "Hey, Lexie?"

"Hey, how did the cheer-weeding go? I mean cheerleading."

Annie didn't want to think about that. "First part was awful, second was pretty good. But that's not why I rang. Listen, how would you like to help me decorate Dad's café?"

"Decorate how?"

Annie paced around the café. Mum did the same thing when she was on the phone; it used to drive Dad crazy. Crazier, rather. "We painted it off-white over the weekend and now have two blank walls in need of some character. Maybe a mural like you did in your room or something? Any ideas?"

"Loads! But wait, are you serious?" Lexie asked.

"Of course. You should see the space. It needs an artist's touch."

"I'll bring sketches to school. Wow, 'K, gotta go. Too many possibilities already. Bye!"

"Bye." Annie hung up and looked around the naked room. Dad was going to love her surprise. Right?

Chapter Seven

Annie watched Tyler and his teammates flirting with the cheerleaders as she waited for Lexie after school. The confidence she felt yesterday after her routine was gone. Even if she made the squad there was no guarantee that Tyler would flirt with her. He was sixteen, an upperclassman. From her few weeks at Liberty Heights, Annie already knew they didn't usually hang out with lowly freshmen.

"Hey, ready?" Lexie came up to her.

Annie sighed and turned away from Tyler and the cheerleaders. "Is it true the cheerleaders don't cheer at the girls' games? That's what a girl on the soccer team in French class was saying."

"Yup," Lexie said. "Same as they don't get pep rallies."

"But why don't they cheer for them?"

Lexie shook her head. "If you're asking that, then maybe cheerleading isn't your thing."

Annie let it go. She kind of knew what Lexie meant. No matter how much people talked about equality and not discriminating, it still happened. Maybe if she made the squad, she could suggest they attend at least a couple of the girls' home games. She didn't see why not. From what she'd heard, the girls' teams were quite good.

"I know something we'd both be into." From her backpack, Annie pulled out the junior roller derby leaflet she took from the bout over the weekend and waved it in front of Lexie. "They have a three-day Fresh Meat programme starting tonight. We should do it together."

Lexie laughed. "Me, a roller girl? Not in this lifetime."

"Aww, come on! Give it a go." Annie pressed her hands together and looked at her with sad eyes. "For me?"

"Stop it." Lexie held up a hand in front of her eyes. "Seriously, me and sports don't mix. I don't even know how to ride a bike. But you could totally rock it."

Annie sighed. She *was* going to try the Fresh Meat, just to see what it was like. But it would be nice to have a friend there doing it with her.

They got to Rosie Lee's and Lexie pulled out her sketchbook so they could look through her ideas. One had black and white geometric figures which Annie thought was a bit too psychedelic. Another was a country landscape with quaint cottages and rolling hills – great sketch, but not right for the café. Turning the next page, Annie knew she'd found it.

"This one. It's perfect." It was a traditional red London double-decker bus filled with very realistic famous British characters and historical figures waving from the windows. Right away Annie recognized the Queen, James Bond, Mary Poppins, Shakespeare, Jane Austin, the Beatles, Robin Hood, Paddington Bear, Naomi Campbell, and Peter Pan who was sitting on top of the bus instead of inside.

Looking at the bus and the "people" in it made Annie's stomach twist. She missed sitting on the upper deck and squealing with her girl friends that the driver was going to crash into the vehicle in front of them. And there was that time she and Dad pretended to be American tourists and asked the driver if he stopped at Hogwarts.

"Ah, who or what is that?" Annie distracted herself by pointing at a green figure in the middle of the bus.

"The Loch Ness Monster!"

"You have Nessie on holiday in London? That's brilliant." Annie laughed.

Lexie grinned, very pleased with herself. "I'm glad you like it, this sketch was my favourite too. Woke me up at two in the morning; artistic brilliance has that tendency. So do bean tacos. Anyway, I'm going to go check my supplies and see what I need to get."

"Would you like some money?" Annie had no idea how much paint cost.

Lexie brushed away the offer. "Are you kidding? This is like having a free art space. It's my dream."

Annie grinned. "All right then. I'll make sure you get a lifetime supply of scones once we're open."

"Deal."

After dinner, Dad drove Annie over to the roller rink in the old white pickup he'd bought off a friend. The building was more than a bit run down with the paint peeling and the roof looking like it had been patched more than once. Most of the lights on the sign were burnt out, so instead of saying "ROCKERS' ROLLER RINK", it only said "O K S L I K".

"Are you sure this is the right place?" Dad asked.

Annie didn't know. "That's what the leaflet said."

They walked in together, Annie with her rollerblades tucked under her arm. The rink was just as shabby on the inside as it was on the outside with faded carpet and chipped plastic food tables. At the far end of the rink near the skate rental booth some girls were getting geared up. A woman with long wavy auburn hair and a Celtic-style tattoo banded around her left bicep skated over the carpet towards them.

"Hi." She held out her hand to shake Annie and Dad's. "Susan Ritter. Are you here for the Fresh Meat workshop?"

Dad straightened his shoulders and ran a hand through his hair, which only make it stick straight up. "Yeah, about that. I'm not really sure if roller derby is the right fit for Annie. I don't want her to get hurt."

Annie was about to argue but Coach Ritter beat her to it. "I completely understand – I have kids too. I'm not going to lie; girls do get hurt sometimes. But I'm a nurse and I make sure we keep a fully stocked first aid kit onsite. No girl is allowed on the rink without proper pads, helmet, and a mouth guard. We take safety very seriously."

Coach Ritter smiled and Dad immediately relented. "I suppose. Annie really wants to try it."

"I really, really do," Annie said.

Coach Ritter nodded. "Part of this Fresh Meat workshop is to get the girls familiar with safety and avoiding injuries, along with the rules. We only use quad skates though. So Annie, why don't you get fitted into skates and pads, while your dad registers you and signs the waiver. You'll need to buy a mouth guard. We don't share those."

Annie thrust her rollerblades into Dad's arms, and headed to the skate rental booth before Dad could change his mind. She stopped short when she saw the cute skater boy she met the first day. His shaggy black hair covered his light blue eyes but he grinned when he saw Annie.

"Hey, I was hoping to see you here. Annie, right?" He pulled out some skates without waiting for Annie to say her size.

Annie blinked and looked over her skates. They weren't pretty: brown and tatty with lots of scratches, but still seemed to be in great working condition. She sat down to try them on.

"That's right. I'm sorry, I don't know your name."

He brushed the hair out of his eyes. "It's Jesse. How do those skates fit?"

Annie wiggled her toes and laced one up. "They're spot on."

Jesse shrugged even though he seemed quite pleased with himself. "I got a knack for anything with wheels. If you don't buy your own, I'll keep these tucked away for you."

"Ta." Annie took the wrist, elbow, and kneepads he held out. Blushing slightly, she looked down from his intense gaze and found herself leaning closer to him instead. She stared at his T-shirt, which had a black and white image of four guys with paper bags over their heads. "Is that The Damned?"

"Yeah, my Velvet Underground T-shirt was dirty. Wait…" He looked up from helping her with her pads. "You actually know The Damned?"

Now it was Annie's turn to shrug. "Of course. 'New Rose' is a classic."

He looked at her as if she were a goddess. "I have *Damned, Damned, Damned* on vinyl."

"Really?" Annie gasped.

"Five bucks at a garage sale," Jesse said.

"I hate you." She grinned.

"All right peeps." Coach Ritter clapped her hands. "Let's get rolling."

Annie buckled the helmet Jesse held out for her and stood up. The last time she was on quad skates was when they were plastic and fitted over her shoe. It was a bit awkward to move in them, but more because she was on the carpet than anything else.

Annie ran her tongue over her top teeth and remembered the guard Coach Ritter had mentioned. Luckily Dad was still where she left him. In his hand was a white container. Annie skated over to him, opened it up, and popped in the blue mouth guard.

"All right there, Dad?" Annie asked. The words came out as if she had a potato in her mouth.

"What? Oh, yeah." He looked away from the skaters warming up in the rink and gave Annie a huge hug. "Be safe."

"I'll be fine. Don't worry," Annie said.

He sighed and kissed the top of her helmet.

Annie watched him leave then turned her attention to the other skaters. Right away she noticed how different everyone looked. In gymnastics, all the girls were similar: short and compact. Here there seemed to be girls of all shapes, sizes, and builds, even one who was close to Annie's height though much heavier.

"Hi, everyone, great to see so many of you," Coach Ritter said with a group of experienced skaters standing behind her smiling encouragingly. Likewise, the roller girls didn't fit one image or mould. Annie recognized a few from school which included the short girl who'd asked the kilt question in English class.

"This workshop is pretty much a skills training, working today on agility and endurance. But really, it's about having a good time. Here to help out are some of the girls in the league. Liz, also known as ElizaDEATH, is a senior and on her fourth year of roller derby."

A tall blonde with broad shoulders and three piercings on each ear gave them two thumbs up.

"Holly Terror, one of our best jammers."

That was the Kilt-Girl from Annie's English class with the fire-engine-red dyed hair. Up close, she was the size of a ten year old but Annie knew she was sixteen. She got onto her toe stops and posed like a model.

Coach Ritter introduced the others and then got down to business.

"We'll start with some stretches, really working on those hip flexors, before warming up. This will be a long and hard training, peeps, so make sure to drink lots of water."

The girls spread out on the rink and crouched down on their skates, straightening out one leg then switching to the other. A heavy girl with spiky blondish-brownish hair was stretching next to Annie.

"Hi, I'm Lauren. You asked me a question in the cafeteria on the first day at school and I still feel bad that I didn't know what you said."

Annie remembered her. She had asked where to queue up and got upset that everyone was making a big deal about her accent. Now with the mouth guard, everyone sounded funny. "I'm sorry if I was rude. That first day was a bit overwhelming."

"I bet." Lauren smiled. Her mouth guard had a leopard-print design. Wicked.

Annie grinned back, glad there were no hard feelings.

They got up from their stretches and Coach Ritter got them

to sprint around the track a couple of times in both directions. The quad skates felt different from Annie's inline ones, her balance was a bit wonky, but even that didn't slow her down too much. She and Lauren were the only two to pass all the other girls before finishing their laps. Annie stretched her right leg out in front to stop. Nothing happened. Except she crashed into the barrier.

Immediately, Liz was at her side. Annie hadn't fallen but the wind had been knocked out of her.

"Are you OK? You're trying to use your heel brake, except there isn't one on quad skates. Happens all the time. Just remember to drag your toe. Great laps though." Liz gave her a friendly pat on the helmet and skated back to the rest.

Next they had to skate backward twice in each direction. Here the quad skates did feel more awkward and it seemed harder to get a good flow. Other "Fresh Meats" were struggling with backward skating too, but Coach Ritter kept shouting out pointers while the girls in the league demonstrated proper technique. When they switched to the other direction, Annie thought about how she skated backwards on the rollerblades and applied that same technique to push off. Much better. Smoother. With a bit of practice, she might catch up with Lauren.

As Coach Ritter set up some cones, Lauren skated up to Annie. "Isn't this great? You have no idea how long I've been waiting to be old enough to play. Now I don't have to take my brother's BS about not being able to play football."

Annie tilted her head to the side and then understood.

American football, of course. "Do boys never play roller derby, then?"

"Not really. I think St Louis is the closest men's team, but it's almost like a different sport; most of them don't have the you-know-whats to wear fishnets and pink bootie shorts."

Annie laughed and turned her attention to the coach.

"Great skating everyone. Now I'm going to have you weave around these cones. I want to see you crouched low, back ends sticking out. That's the skater stance and I want everyone in that position all the time. You're down, you're grounded. You're up, you might as well be on the floor. Holly, why don't you show them?"

Holly skated towards them, spun around to change direction, kept skating backward and then got on her toe stops right in front of them.

"So, you know those gross public bathrooms you really don't want to sit on? You want to get low enough so you don't pee on the seat, but not so close that you catch something vile."

There was a collective cringe from the girls as they imagined those public toilets. They watched Holly zip around the cones, crouched low, like it was the easiest thing. As they tried it out themselves, everyone shouted out suggestions and encouragement. Annie couldn't get over how supportive everyone was.

"That was good fun," Annie said when she skated back to Lauren.

"You're a natural. I bet you'll make the team."

"If anyone makes it, it'll be you. I barely know the rules

or anything."

"C'mon, guys." Holly had overheard them. "It takes more than one day to become a roller girl, and even then we're all still learning."

She had a point. Annie's gymnastics trainer always said that if you thought you knew everything about something, you knew nothing.

Liz, perhaps inspired by Annie's crash, taught them how to stop. "The easiest way is to drag and press down on one of your toes. You can also do a snowplough with your legs wide and bringing your toes together like a V. This is really, really useful when you're blocking in the pack. Makes you more solid. Just don't let your legs go too far apart or you'll end up doing a really painful splits."

The girls laughed at Liz's mock splits and her pained expression that seemed to be taken from experience. Liz laughed with them as she straightened up.

"If you feel more confident, you can try the T-stop," she continued. "One skate forward and the other behind it to make an upside-down T. The wheels on that back skate scrape against the ground to make you stop. Warning, don't let the wheels touch the other skate or you'll wipe-out."

"What about that one Holly does?" one of the girls asked.

On cue, Holly skated over, turned backward, and skidded to a stop on her toes. A few girls clapped as Holly gave a little curtsy.

Liz nodded. "That's the tomahawk stop. Don't try it unless you're really good at switching from forward to backward. And try it slow the first few times."

They practised the various stops. Annie mastered the basic toe drag and T-stop on both sides. The snowplough she knew from skiing holidays in France, but never felt it was a pretty stop. She practised it anyway, just because Liz said it was useful. With a deep breath, Annie tried Holly's flashy tomahawk stop. She barely had enough momentum to turn from forward to backward but she did it! Next time, she would up her speed from slug to turtle.

The last thing Coach Ritter got them to do was play a "game" of Red Light, Green Light. "It's simple. When I say 'green light', you go, when I say 'red light', you stop. If you move without a green light, you go back to start. If you fall, pick yourself up and keep going. First one to cross the finish line wins. OK, girls, places."

The girls crouched behind the line, one skate forward and hand on knee.

"Ready … green light!"

They dashed down for less than two seconds when Coach Ritter shouted, "Red light!"

Annie stopped using the T-stop she'd just learned and almost lost her balance. But almost wasn't the same as actually losing it. With a few funky chicken moves, Annie managed to stay on her skates. Two of girls weren't that lucky and landed with a thump that had them both moaning. But, laughing, they helped each other up before Coach Ritter shouted the next green light.

Halfway to the finish line and Annie was in the lead with

Lauren right behind her. That's when Coach started getting cheeky. She got Lauren to return to the start with "green lettuce".

"And that's why I hate vegetables." Lauren skated back to the start but with a good-natured smile. With every stop, Annie felt more confident and more in control of her skates.

"Green tomatoes … green onions … green light!

Annie sprinted a few good strides before having to dig in her toe to stop. The rest of the crowd was a good three metres behind her.

Coach tried a different tactic. "I was driving the other day, saw a green car parked outside a green house. It was at a junction with a green light—"

Didn't work. As soon as she heard light, Annie was off.

A metre from the finish, Coach almost got Annie with "red robin" but gut feeling told her to keep skating even though she heard "red". Annie crossed the line and threw her arms in the air in victory. Everyone congratulated her, and some of them, including Lauren and Liz, gave her hugs. There were no sour grapes, no condescending fake smiles from anyone. Everyone was genuinely happy for her.

Annie unbuckled her helmet to wipe the sweat from her forehead. Now that was brilliant. Tiring, but oh so cool. She couldn't wait until the next practice.

Chapter Eight

Before classes started the next day Annie overheard two girls crying in the bathrooms. They hadn't made the cheerleading callbacks.

"I checked the notice on the board like ten times. I can't believe they didn't want me," one of them sobbed into her hands.

"My life is totally ruined now," the other one wailed.

Callbacks? The only "board" Annie knew of was the one next to the principal's office. Annie headed over there feeling a bit confused. Why hadn't anyone bothered to let her know the callbacks had been posted? Unless she hadn't made it…

Or unless she had and someone was hoping she wouldn't show up.

She ran her finger down the names. Had she made it? Yes!

There she was: Annie Turner.

Her name was with nine other girls, no guys. Callbacks, this afternoon. Not only did she not know the list had been posted, no one had told her that the callbacks would be today after school.

And she had nothing with her to wear.

Dad. He could bring her something. After all, he was the one really pushing the whole cheerleading thing. Not that she was trying out for him; she had to see it through for herself. She wasn't a quitter.

She headed to her locker for the morning's books and found Lexie there. Today she was wearing authentic bell-bottom trousers, a real tie-dyed shirt, and lots of homemade beaded jewellery. And a huge grin.

"Checked my supplies and we're set to paint that bus whenever," Lexie said.

Annie put the cheerleading callbacks out of her mind. "Brilliant. How about tonight? Dad's going out to play basketball so he won't be around to ask what we're doing."

"He doesn't know?" Lexie asked.

Annie could just picture his smile when he saw it. "I really want to surprise him. How long do you think it'll take?"

"Few hours, I bet. We might not have enough time to do it all today. Mom insists I get home by eight-thirty on weekdays. She's convinced the predators start roaming the streets at eight-thirty-one."

"What if you stayed the night?" Annie asked. "Dad won't mind, my friends used to do it all the time in London."

82

"Let me ask." While Lexie called her mom, Jesse came over. He pulled off his large DJ headphones and grinned.

"Hey, how ya feeling after the Fresh Meat workshop?"

Annie rubbed her legs and moaned. "I'm aching all over. It's like I've never used my thighs and bum before! And there are muscles on my back I didn't even know I had." She broke into a huge smile and added, "But I love it; it's such fun and the girls are really nice."

Jesse nodded as if Annie had just complimented his sisters. "Coach Ritter is real good. She was a great jammer, Miss Demeanour, before a shoulder injury made her retire. The Illinoisies won most of their championships because of her. She'll make you work but she really knows her stuff."

"She seemed great."

Lexie got off the phone. "Mom said yes. Paint party!"

"Brilliant," Annie said, then explained to Jesse, "We're decorating my dad's café tonight."

"Sweet. What's the theme?"

Annie explained the bus to Jesse and turned to Lexie. "Shall I ring when I've finished?"

"You do know that callbacks are *this* afternoon, right?" a rude voice interrupted loudly. Kelsey stopped right in front of Annie with her two matching minions on either side.

No thanks to you. "Yes, I know."

"What callbacks?" Jesse asked.

"Cheer-weeding," Lexie muttered. Jesse crossed his arms and leaned against the lockers.

Kelsey ignored Annie's friends as if they didn't exist. "In case you actually make the squad, you should know you're not just a cheerleader during the games, you're a cheerleader *all* the time."

Annie turned her attention away from her friends to focus on Kelsey. "I don't understand?"

Kelsey sighed as if she were explaining something simple to a toddler for the umpteenth time. Her minions rolled their eyes in unison. "It means that cheerleaders represent the school. People will expect you to *look* like a cheerleader, not some London freak."

Kelsey gave a sound of disgust as she glanced up and down at Annie. Unlike Kelsey whose purple designer shirt and short suit looked like it came off the catwalk (her minions were sporting similar outfits), Annie was wearing her favourite Sex Pistols T-shirt and jeans. There was nothing designer about her clothes except that it was a genuine Sex Pistols T-shirt and not some knock-off.

Jesse shifted his weight. He was just a bit taller than Annie but just as skinny and not very intimidating. "Is that supposed to be an insult? Freak? Seriously, is that the best you can do?"

Lexie turned to him. "Brain waves are very painful for her."

Annie bit her lip. Laughing at the cheerleading captain might not be the best idea.

Kelsey pretended not to hear, though her voice was considerably louder as she continued to talk to Annie. "You should really think about who you hang out with. And not such…" Kelsey looked at Jesse and Lexie up and down. "Alternative types."

"Yeah, Annie. You really should think about it," Lexie said

with a mock serious expression.

"Alternative to what?" Jesse asked, looking amused. "A penguin?"

Kelsey ignored them, a clear sign that she either couldn't think of a comeback fast enough or didn't get their sarcasm. She just turned on her high heel with her minions behind her, though one, Lulu, let out a "humph" before leaving.

Jesse pushed his hair back and gave Annie a puzzled look. "You want to be a cheerleader? With her as captain?"

Annie tried to shrug it off even though the look on Jesse's face was the same as it would be if he discovered Annie was a flesh-eating alien. Sure Kelsey was rude and annoying, but that couldn't be true of all the cheerleaders. The pep rally had been loads of fun, their uniform was really nice, and most of all, now that Annie started the try-outs she wasn't going to quit. "I'm quite good at gymnastics."

"I never thought of you as the cheerleading type." Jesse put on his headphones and walked off.

Lexie sighed as if she wasn't surprised at Jesse's response. Annie sighed too. Her school in London had its cliques, of course, but Annie never felt that if she was a gymnast she couldn't be friends with someone from a different group. Just because she wanted to be a cheerleader, didn't mean she was going to start acting like Kelsey. There had to be another "alternative", right?

* * *

Annie had to borrow clothes from lost and found; Dad was dealing with suppliers and wasn't able to bring her leotard to school for the try-out. The options weren't too great. She settled for a pair of boys' long basketball shorts and a shirt she chose to wear inside out or it would have read "Hooters". It was the beginning of the school year, there was nothing else that fit.

Annie knew she had to make the most of it – there wasn't anything she could do about it. She wasn't Dad, who'd have a laugh while wearing odd clothes.

As soon as Annie walked into the gym, it struck her how everyone looked alike, both the cheerleaders and hopefuls. Of course there were racial differences, but everyone was slim and pretty. Just by being a little taller than the other girls, Annie felt like she stood out.

And the borrowed clothing didn't help.

Not that she wanted to look like them, but she wished there was more diversity in appearances.

Like in roller derby.

"OK, girls," the coach said. "You're here because you stood out in the try-outs. Unfortunately, we only have room for four of you on the squad. So make sure you give it all you got."

As soon as she said that, the girls stepped away from each other. Almost as if they were afraid the others would ruin their chances of making it by being too close.

Kelsey came up to them and burst out laughing when she saw Annie's outfit. "Looks like the circus is in town."

Annie looked down. If only she could disappear, after taking a mighty swing at Kelsey.

I'm not going to let her get to me. I'm going to hit her where it hurts. By getting into the squad.

Kelsey taught them a new dance routine to an even more disturbingly catchy pop song than the one she played the week before. With every movement Annie could feel the soreness in her muscles from yesterday's roller derby. Not that it bothered her. It was a nice reminder of a great night and how friendly everyone had been.

Unlike the callback. There was no friendliness from anyone. It was every girl for herself.

One girl lost her balance during a turn and accidentally stepped on Kelsey's toes.

"You nearly broke my foot, you cow!" Kelsey yelled. "I can't believe you. Only a total clutz would do that." She dramatically limped off to one side to sit down. Immediately Kelsey's second in commands hovered next to her.

The poor girl looked ready to burst into tears. Annie narrowed her eyes. She'd seen the misstep and really couldn't believe it hurt that much.

Had she been a roller girl, she would have laughed and helped the girl up. Unlikely. This was Kelsey, she'd never be a roller girl. Granted, if she were, maybe she'd be nicer.

"Watch where you're going, girls," the coach said. "And smile. Big, mouth-hurting smiles. If you're not hurting, you're not smiling enough."

Annie spread her lips as far as they'd go. It wasn't as bad

as the other times, but it didn't reach her eyes. She wanted to make the squad. Whether it was because she was competitive or actually wanted to be a cheerleader, she didn't know any more. But even if she did a perfect callback, would Kelsey ever let her on the squad?

Lexie was waiting for her at Rosie Lee's with a small overnight bag and another bag large enough to fit a body. "Art supplies. I had Dad drop me off. Can you imagine me hauling that the half a mile from my house to here?"

Annie laughed. "Not really."

She pulled out the keys Dad had given her and they both dragged the body bag into the café. Lexie looked around the space again and took a deep breath as if she couldn't believe her dream had come true. "Are you sure your dad will like it?"

"Ninety-six per cent," Annie said. "And if he doesn't, I'll paint over it."

Lexie whimpered at the thought, then seemed to accept the possibility. "There are always lost masterpieces in every artist's life. Remind me to take a picture before we leave, just in case."

Annie switched on the old radio in the kitchen while Lexie sketched the outline of the bus. Even with just the faint lines on the wall, the café felt as if it were coming alive.

"That looks amazing," Annie said as Lexie started mixing paints.

"How good are your art skills?" Lexie asked, handing her a brush and a tray with red paint.

"I can paint within the lines, is that good enough?" Annie said, her hand already itching to get started. Dad was going to love it. He had to.

"Perfect. The bus is all yours while I do the people. Once you're done, I'll touch it up a bit. Groovy?"

"Sure, Michelangelo," Annie teased. Who knows? Comparing Rosie Lee's to the Sistine Chapel might not be that much of a stretch once Lexie worked her magic.

"I like him. Wait, you're talking about the ninja turtle, right?" Lexie joked as she sketched out bus passengers. "Shame there are no real famous British superheroes for the bus. I mean there's Captain Britain I guess, but no one but comic book nerds like me have heard of him."

Annie couldn't think of any either. Though that wasn't to say there weren't some cool British characters with special powers. "I'm glad you have David Tennant as Doctor Who."

"Course. He's the hottest and he had Martha. I used to pretend I was her. Time and space travel would be so cool."

Annie nodded, it would be interesting that's for sure. "I don't fancy meeting some of those aliens though."

"It's not like they'd be worse than the ones we already know." Lexie said as she did the outline for Nessie.

Annie knew by Lexie's grin that she wasn't talking about the green monsters from space with three eyes, but she couldn't work out the reference. "Which aliens?"

"The cheerleaders, of course. I'm sure you figured out by now they're not human."

Annie laughed but inside she was worried. She hoped Lexie was just teasing and that she wouldn't pull a Jesse if she did become a cheerleader.

Chapter Nine

"Dad! Dad!" Annie and Lexie burst into the kitchen where Dad was enjoying his coffee and croissants still hot from the oven.

"What's the matter?" Dad asked, putting down his coffee.

"We've overslept and you have to drive us to school, right now." Annie squeezed Lexie's hand, barely able to hold in her excitement.

Dad looked at his watch. "You still have plenty of time."

"No, you see the thing is I left my school bag at Rosie Lee's and there's this bit of homework…" Annie stopped, afraid she was digging herself into hole she couldn't get out of.

Dad got up from the chair. "OK, calm down. Let me get the keys."

"And shoes," Annie reminded him.

"Shoes, snooze." But when Dad came back he was wearing his trainers, one of them still covered in paint. Annie and Lexie each grabbed a couple of croissants before following him out to the truck. The girls squeezed in next to Dad.

Dad sighed as he turned the key. "It's not like you to be so forgetful, Beanie. I think you've been hanging around me too much."

"No, it's just with school and cheerleading and roller derby and stuff, I forgot." Annie stared at Lexie in the hope she'd help her out but Lexie was biting her lip to stop herself from laughing.

"Stuff? Is that teen-speak for 'boy'?"

The girls burst out laughing, which made Dad think he was right. No point in correcting him. He'd find out soon enough.

Dad parked the truck in front of the café. "I'll wait for you."

"No, I left my keys," Annie said. How were they going to get him to come in without revealing the surprise?

Dad turned off the truck and got out with a grumble. "Next time, I might think twice about letting you have a sleepover on a weekday."

He unlocked the door and turned on the lights. The whole café burst alive with the characters on the bus. Last night when they finished, Annie thought it looked good. Now with the sunlight coming in through the front windows, the sight was spectacular. Every character on the bus was cartoony but instantly recognizable.

"Surprise!" Annie said.

Dad was speechless. He went up to the wall and touched

Sherlock Holmes's face to convince himself he was really seeing him.

"Do you like it?" Annie asked, suddenly thinking it wasn't such a good idea. Dad being quiet for a long time was never a good sign.

Dad went from one person to the next, identifying them as he went along. "It's incredible. Who did this and how much do I owe them?"

Annie let out the breath she had been holding and grinned. "Nothing. It was all Lexie's idea."

"Not true," Lexie said. "Annie wanted to spice up the place. I just did the art."

Dad wrapped Annie in a big hug, and then pulled Lexie in too. "It's perfect, beautiful. Lexie, you are incredibly talented. You're like a modern-day Andy Warhol."

"I wish," Lexie said.

Dad let go of them and looked over the mural in greater detail. He turned back to them with a big frown. "I'm afraid there's a problem."

"What?" Annie asked.

Dad crossed his arms and tapped his paint-covered trainer. "You didn't sign it, Lexie. Art is worth nothing if it's not signed."

Lexie laughed and pulled a green marker from her bag to sign the right bottom corner with her full name: Alexis Raquel Jones.

Dad beamed. "Now it's perfect. Except I better get you two to school before you really *are* late."

* * *

At first the day got even better. After English class, Tyler came up to Annie's desk. He hadn't done that since the first day. Yes he smiled and waved when they saw each other in passing but Annie assumed they were just "hi" friends. Not "coming over to her desk for a chat" friends.

"Hey." Tyler leaned over as she gathered her books. "Did you get that homework? Writing an essay on the current 'tone' of *Two Cities*. What does she want?"

Annie licked her lips. She knew what Ms Schwartz meant, but how could she explain it? Especially when Tyler made her get all muddled up just by being around. "Uh, I think we have to write about the mood so far in the book. Is it happy, sad, sarcastic, that sort of thing."

Tyler nodded. "That sounds doable. Hey, how did the cheerleading callbacks work out?"

Annie blinked. He knew she'd been called back? Just the thought made butterflies do backflips in her stomach. "Not too bad."

"I love how you say that, 'Not too baahhd.' Your accent is really cute, you know?"

Instead of bothering her, like it did when everyone else pointed out her accent, Tyler's comment made her insides flip-flop more. Did he really think her accent was cute, or was that his way of saying he thought she was cute?

"Well, American accents can be quite cute—" Annie

94

started to say until Kelsey sashayed her way right between them. For once she was on her own, her clones obviously on mental-health leave.

"Tyler, did I tell you how great your penalty shot was over the weekend? How did you do it?" Kelsey linked her arm through Tyler's and fluttered her eyelashes at him.

Tyler beamed as he recapped his goal. "Well, the first thing is to fake out the goalie…" The two of them walked away to their next class. Tyler seemed to have forgotten all about Annie. Kelsey didn't. She turned around and mouthed to Annie, "Mine," before laughing at whatever Tyler had said.

So much for the morning's good mood.

As Annie finished her essay on the tone of *A Tale of Two Cities*, she'd come to two conclusions: she had to be more assertive and she had to start going to soccer games at school. It was the only way she would have a chance with Tyler.

"M'lady, might I interrupt?" Dad said in an old-fashioned accent.

Annie saved the document and closed the lid of the computer. The essay was done and she could double-check it before class tomorrow just to be sure. She was at Rosie Lee's with Dad trying to sort out the menu and testing the new kitchen equipment.

"I'm afraid if you must." Annie straightened herself and pretended she was the mistress of a grand estate. Much easier than working out how to be assertive.

Dad bowed. "M'lady, might I offer you a sample of this year's harvest?"

"That depends. Of what harvest do you speak?" Lady Anne peered upon the manservant with distaste.

The manservant revealed a tray from behind his back and placed it in front of Lady Anne. "If it pleases, m'lady, I have before me a new-fangled meal brought to my attention by the Earl of Sandwich himself."

Lady Anne peered at the mounds of bread suspiciously. "And what, pray tell, are in these concoctions?"

"Only the finest, choosiest ingredients for m'lady." The manservant pointed to each mini sandwich individually. "Tender ham and Dutch gouda cheese laced with apple sauce. Shaved turkey and fresh mozzarella with pesto and toe-mah-toe. And finally roasted mushrooms with chèvre from the local caprine dairy and avocado imported from the land of California."

Lady Anne waved her hand in distaste. "That shan't do. I will only consume avocados from the land of Florida. You know that. Now take them away."

"Very good, m'lady." The manservant bobbed his head and picked up the tray to head back to the kitchen.

"Oh, bring it back, you." Annie dropped her act. "I thought you were going to serve British food: shepherd's pie, bangers and mash, roast beef and Yorkshire pudding, things like that."

Dad set the tray back on the opening between the dining area and kitchen that Annie had been using as a homework table.

"I figured it'd be best to start with pastries and sandwiches, which I can make ahead of time, and see how it goes. If I do hot meals, I'll have to hire someone. I've tried to be in two places at once. Doesn't work." Dad sighed.

That made sense, though it was still a shame. Dad's roast beef and Yorkshire pudding was Annie's absolute favourite.

"All right, then. Let's see what you've got." Annie reached for the first sandwich, ham, cheese, and apple sauce. Surprisingly gorgeous. The turkey was good, of course. And the last one with avocado and goat's cheese was pure heaven.

"So you really think people will buy them?" Dad stuffed his hands into his apron to hide how nervous he was.

"Dad, you can take on Gordon Ramsey anytime, plus you're loads friendlier. Rosie Lee's is going to be a hit. I know it." Annie finished off the rest of the sandwiches.

Dad hugged her and planted a kiss on the top of her head. "You're a great daughter."

"I'm just being honest."

"I know. That's what makes you so great. Let's go, it's almost derby time."

At the rink, Annie and Lauren were the first ones to put on all their gear and start warming up with figure eights. Jesse seemed pleased to see Annie when she collected her skates though he didn't say much. Like he was reserving judgment about cheerleaders until he knew how Annie would turn out.

"All right, peeps, gather round for a sec." Coach Ritter waved them all to the centre of the rink. "First of all, I'm so glad to see you; we've had a few girls decide not to come back and I wish them well. Today we're mainly going to work on blocking. This is a contact sport so everyone needs to know how to block. If you can't block, you can't be a jammer. Simple as that. To get you ready for that, you'll need to know how to push your way through the pack."

Coach Ritter quickly counted the Fresh Meat and her roller girls. "OK, in groups of four. How many of you like shopping?"

About half the girls raised their hands and some, like Annie, half held theirs up, not willing to fully commit until they knew what was going on.

"Right, well we're doing a different kind of shopping today with a drill called Shopping Carts. Groups, choose who's going first."

Annie was put in the group with Liz and two girls whose names Annie had forgotten. The one with glasses said she wanted to go first.

"Now line up, single file, and hold onto the hips of the girl in front. Whoever's at the back has to push the line of girls to the other end of the rink. I want everyone crouched real low, knees bent, booties out. Ready … go!"

Annie's first thought was that it was kind of fun having someone else making her go. But then as the girl in the back went faster, it was harder for her to control the "cart" and make sure they went in a straight line. Not that that made it less fun. At one point they did a complete 360-degree turn that had them all laughing. When it was Annie's turn, she remembered those wonky shopping trolleys back home that never went the way you wanted them to go. And also three people on wheels was still a heavy amount to push. The game was fun and everyone enjoyed the craziness. Getting on her toe stops helped to get the other girls moving. She could feel the effort in her thighs and bum as she leaned and pushed them towards the finish line.

Coach Ritter clapped as the final group pushed their "shopping cart" to the "designated area".

"Good job, everyone, good job. Keep in mind you can use a variant of that in an actual jam. Your own teammates can be props. You can grab her by the hips or grip her arm to whip around the pack. That's totally legal. You can even roll over her back if the opportunity is there. Just don't knock her down or use the other team as a prop."

A few girls let out scared chuckles. Annie sympathized; she knew what was coming next.

Blocking. Oh joy.

When she saw the Illinoisies play, Annie kept imagining herself as a jammer. She was fast, agile, and lean. Blocking might just break her. But if she couldn't block, she'd never become a jammer.

"We're covering bootie-blocking today. This is your biggest blocking asset, if you get what I'm saying." Coach Ritter patted her backside. "Keep looking over your shoulders – you want to know where the jammers are all the time. Stay low, like we've been practising. In pairs, one girl is going to bootie-block the other who's trying to get around her. I don't want to see any grabbing or elbow blocking," Coach Ritter warned as she paired them up.

Lauren was first and paired up with one of the girls in the league, Mattie. Lauren seemed to know exactly what to do and really set the standard for blocking. Her size helped, but she was also quick and had her bum swinging back and forth as she skated from one side to the other. Her head snapped from one shoulder to look over the other, never caught off guard.

"Yeah, Lauren!" Liz cheered and everyone else joined in to cheer her on. One girl, Aiko, whistled loudly. Annie clapped until her hands hurt.

When it was time for Lauren and Mattie to switch roles, Lauren hadn't allowed the experienced girl to pass her once. She was certain to get into the team.

Three more pairs went before it was Annie's turn. She was paired up with Holly.

"Pass or block first?" Holly asked.

From what Annie had seen, neither seemed like something she could do.

"Ah, pass please," Annie whispered.

Annie crouched down, feeling like a giant next to an ant. But maybe that was a good thing; Holly couldn't be too hard to pass.

Wrong.

Annie was vaguely aware of people cheering and the coach

shouting suggestions, but she couldn't really hear them. Holly was right in front of her and every time Annie tried to get around her, Holly swung her bum around to keep her from passing.

Think assertive. See a gap and go for it. Fake her out.

Annie sprinted to the side, changed directions, and then immediately changed back to the original side. For the smallest second, she thought she had made it. But no. Holly wasn't fooled. Changing the angle of her skates, she cut across the track and was at Annie's side in an instant. With a big swing of her hips, she made contact with Annie's side. Annie's skates left the ground. Not just her skates, all of her. She was in the air, flying. She reached out, trying to grab onto something … anything…

Before landing on her back with a loud thump.

Chapter Ten

"Are you crazy?"

Annie blinked. It took a second for her eyes to focus. A few more to understand what she was seeing. She was on the floor of the rink, staring at a ceiling fan going round and round. Holly was at her side. Also on the ground. No, not any more. She got up, rubbing her bum. It was a few more seconds before Annie realized Holly was the one talking.

If you could call it that.

"Never, ever grab another girl and bring her down! Never!" Holly screamed. "Grabbing like that can cause a pile-up and get you kicked out of the bout."

"I'm so sorry. Are you OK?" Annie eased herself up to sitting, feeling a bit light-headed. Thank goodness for helmets.

"No, but I'll live." Holly skated off, not showing any signs of an injury other than a face that matched her fire-engine hair.

Annie stayed sitting on the rink a few seconds longer until Coach Ritter dashed to her side and dropped to her knees. "Annie, honey, look in my eyes. Can you move?"

Annie stared at the coach's green eyes. She was still a little dazed. One minute she was about to zip by Holly and the next they were both on the ground. "I think so."

Coach Ritter checked her over, paying special attention to her spine and head. Her back was hurt and her elbows were really sore even though the pads had taken the brunt of the fall. At least everything seemed to still work. When the coach finished the examination, she jerked her head to one of the girls. "Liz, help me get her off the rink."

The two helped her up and kept their arms around her as they skated off. Annie could feel the spot where Holly had blocked her on the thigh and knew there was going to be a huge bruise. Despite being so small, Holly could certainly hit hard. Still, Annie started feeling self-conscious with all the attention she was getting. Holly had fallen too, and no one was helping her off the rink.

They helped her onto a threadbare bench, double-checked she was all right, and skated back onto the rink. Immediately, Jesse was next to her with a bottle of cold orange juice. Any concern that Annie might suddenly turn into a stuck-up cheerleader was gone from his face.

"That was some wipe-out." He looked at her up and down,

half concerned and half impressed.

"That floor is really, really hard." Annie drank her juice as she watched the rest of the girls going through their blocking.

A few kept giving her worried looks. Twice Lauren mouthed, "Are you OK?"

"The first major fall is always the worst. But now you're initiated as a real roller girl. Every fall will just make you better. Build character." Jesse pointed to the faint scar above his right eye. "Wiped-out on a half-pipe, board tip hit me square in the head."

"That's awful."

Jesse grinned. "Six stitches."

Annie finished her juice and stood up. She was glad that she and Jesse were cool again but hated all the attention she was getting from everyone. It was like they didn't think she was tough enough to handle a fall. "I'm going back. Thanks for the juice."

She threw the bottle into the recycling and skated back onto the rink. Her hip and thigh ached every time she used that leg, her back felt like it had been slapped by a giant hand, and her elbows would have broken if she hadn't been wearing pads, but none of it was serious. Nothing to keep her from continuing on with the training. No one could call Annie Turner a quitter.

Coach Ritter nodded her approval when she saw Annie back in the group. "Now's probably a good time to cover falling. If you've taken martial arts, you probably learned to tuck and roll. That's fine as long as you don't roll into anyone. Think 'fall small'. Keeps you and the others safe. What I'm going to teach you is to fall forward whenever possible. That's where your pads are. That's where you're most protected."

She asked Liz and Holly to demonstrate a block and a fall. Holly blocked and Liz faked a fall, landing squarely on her hands and knees. A second later, Liz was back on her skates.

"That's your four-point fall. You can also aim to land on your elbows or forearms," Coach Ritter said. "Whenever you fall, get up as soon as you can and keep skating."

That's where I went wrong. That's why they were fussing over me. I just sat there like a weakling instead of getting up. Next time, Annie knew, things were going to be different. Now that she knew what to expect, she wouldn't be so dazed.

Liz blocked Holly this time and Holly dropped to one knee, got back up, and fell on the other knee. She made the move, which Coach Ritter called taking a knee, look so graceful it reminded Annie of figure skaters.

Two other girls, Sam and Keisha, demonstrated the baseball slide. As you weren't landing straight on the leg but rather at an angle, it didn't hurt that much. So they said.

The last fall they showed was a simple double knee drop that Coach Ritter called the "rock star" fall. From her knees, the girl brought her toe stops under her and used them to get herself up and off down the rink.

Once demonstrated, Coach Ritter set up cones in each corner and had the Fresh Meat skate around the rink performing a different fall in each corner.

"Get comfortable with the falls. Don't be afraid of them.

Now is *not* a time to communicate – don't announce you're falling. If someone falls in front of you, it's your responsibility to avoid her. You need to be prepared to clear any obstacles in your way."

Annie tried all the falls a few times and wished Coach Ritter had thought to show them how to fall before blocking; Holly made a big show of staying clear of Annie. In terms of falling, Annie found the four-point the most efficient but the one knee was still the prettiest and for nothing other than vanity, Annie wanted to spend more time perfecting it. The baseball slide wasn't too bad after all, but she didn't dare try it on her sore side. That could wait for another day. The best part was that now that she knew how to fall, she wouldn't bring anyone down with her again. She didn't need any more enemies.

When they had finished the falling drills, most of the girls were panting, but everyone seemed to be pretty pleased with themselves.

"Great job, everyone. I'm really proud." Coach Ritter looked at them all in turn. "You've all come so far. Now tomorrow I'll be giving you a skills test, to see how much you've learned. It's not a competition and I hate making you do it, but the fact is that if you can't perform these skills, it's not safe for you to play. However, if you sign up for more training and keep practising, I'll welcome anyone, anytime you pass. In my book, roller derby is about accepting, not selecting. Stretch and cool down."

As soon as Annie took off her skates and pads, she lifted her shorts to check out the bruise on her thigh. About ten centimetres wide and more than a little purple. Just brushing against it as she shifted her shorts was painful.

"Ooh, that's a beauty." Lauren peered at Annie's bruise. "You should ice it once you get home."

Annie eased her shorts back in place with a moan. "Good idea."

"Derby isn't for the prim and proper, Princess Kate," Holly said as she walked by with her equipment bag.

Annie pressed her lips together. It wasn't the first time someone had said she looked a bit like Kate Middleton, but this time it sounded like an insult. "Kate is actually a duchess."

As soon as the words left her mouth, she realized how silly and childish she sounded.

Holly scowled. "Like I care. This is a hard-core sport. If you can't hack it, don't bother."

Annie wasn't complaining about her sore spots, no one here could say they'd heard her complaining. If anything, she was admiring the damage. The last time she had such a big bruise was when she missed her footing after a tuck and landed sideways on the balance beam. Just because she was English didn't mean she wasn't tough. The English created rugby after all, that was hard core and tough. Tomorrow during the skills test, she'd prove she was too.

Lauren seemed to know what she was thinking and gave her a friendly punch on the shoulder before leaving. "You did great."

Lauren high-fived the roller girls as if she were already part of the team and swaggered out of the building. The roller girls talked and laughed with each other as they headed out.

Annie's stomach tightened. They belonged. They were all part of a group. Last time Annie felt like that was at the West London Gymnastics Centre. Oh god, how she missed that lot: Nicola, Georgie, and Mel. It seemed like such a long time ago – such a long time since she fitted in *and* was part of a group of friends.

Back at home with an ice pack on her leg, Annie fired up the computer. Maybe one of her mates had emailed her. Maybe there was some news or mention of how much they missed her. No, but there was an email from Mum:

Annie, I'm working all night on this case. If you get a chance, Skype me so we can have a chat. Miss you!

Mum

Annie looked at the Skype icon and sure enough her mum was online even though it was after three in the morning in London.

Before she could do anything, the computer was flashing and ringing with a call from Philippa Bradley.

Annie gulped. Bradley. Mum had gone back to her maiden name. It made the separation seem final.

"Hi, Mum." Annie pulled on her headphones. Through the wall that separated her room from Dad's she could hear him snoring already.

"Annie, sweetheart, how are you?" Mum adjusted the screen so the camera had her centred. Her shoulder-length light-brown hair had been re-dyed a darker shade since the last time they'd talked.

"Fine, tired." Annie shifted the ice pack, glad her mum couldn't see what she was doing.

Still Mum's blue eyes narrowed. "What's wrong? Is your father running you ragged getting that silly café ready?"

"No, nothing like that. It's just…" Annie paused. It was usually Dad with whom she normally talked about these things, not Mum. "I miss you, I miss all my friends. I miss a good cuppa. I miss being in a place I know, and belong."

"Oh, sweetheart, I'm sorry. I miss you too. Did something happen?"

"No, not really," Annie sighed. "It's just that I'm trying out to be a cheerleader, but my friends don't like cheerleaders, just because the captain is a bit of a pain."

"It's always difficult when friends don't get along," Mum sympathized. "But ultimately, if they don't like you just for being a cheerleader, then they're not really your friends."

Annie knew Mum was right but didn't want to think about that. She liked Lexie and Jesse a lot already and didn't want to say goodbye. And anyway, she was probably worrying about it for no reason. Kelsey hated her, so was likely to do everything she could to keep Annie off the cheerleading squad. "Yes, I know."

"And what about that roller skating thing you were telling me about?"

Annie straightened up, feeling the stiffness from landing on her back. Even so, a huge grin spread across her face. "It's so much fun, and the girls are brilliant." Except maybe Holly. "But I still feel like an outsider."

Mum nodded, pushing her glasses up her nose. "You know, you can come back here. I can make all the arrangements, talk to your headmistress, won't be any trouble at all. What do you think?"

Annie didn't know what to think. She was only saying how she felt, she hadn't meant that she wanted to go back. Did she?

She shifted the ice pack again and stretched out her elbows. Even if she didn't get into the roller derby team, she'd miss the friends she had already made. She scratched a bit of red paint off her finger left from the mural at the café. She would really miss Lexie. And Rosie Lee's grand opening. And Dad. She couldn't leave Dad.

On cue, Dad gave a loud snore through the wall and then was silent.

Maybe she hadn't given Liberty Heights a fair chance.

"Thanks, Mum, but I'll stay here for now. I'm not ready to give up on America just yet." *Besides*, Annie thought with a pang of sadness, *it's not like I'm still part of my gymnastics group. I'll feel like an outsider in London too.*

Mum sighed and suddenly seemed very tired. "Well, give it a think and let me know if you change your mind. I really miss you and would love to have you back here with me."

"Thanks, Mum. I miss you too."

"I better let you go. If I finish this paperwork soon, I might get two hours of sleep."

"Don't work too hard. Love you," Annie said.

Mum blew a kiss at the screen. "I love you too, sweetheart."

The screen went dark and Annie let out a big breath. What would it be like living with Mum? It wouldn't be that bad, would it? Look how much Mum wanted her back. It could work. Maybe. Or maybe not.

Annie knew half of the reason they were getting along so well now was because they were living thousands of miles apart.

Chapter Eleven

Annie wrapped the towel around herself the next morning after her shower and headed to her room to get dressed for school.

"Annie Turner, what is that on your leg?" Dad gasped.

Annie twisted around and noticed a giant black and blue bruise on her thigh. She shrugged it off. "I'm fine. It barely hurts any more."

Dad crossed his arms. "Right, and I married Pinocchio's mother."

"Dad, I—"

"Don't 'Dad' me. This is serious. I really don't think this roller derby thing is a good idea. That is a nasty bruise. Do you have more like that one?"

Annie hugged the towel tighter around her. He couldn't make

her give up derby, he couldn't. "I'm fine, really. And I know how to fall now so it probably won't happen again. Jesse says the first fall is always the worst."

"The first fall? You mean it happens a lot?"

Annie bit her lip. The sport was played on roller skates and a big part involved blocking each other. There were bound to be falls. And many of them. "It's not as bad as it sounds."

Dad paced around in a circle, pulling his hair straight up like an arch over his head, and then sighed. "Don't you find out about cheerleading today? That does seem like the better choice. Less hazardous."

He obviously hadn't met Kelsey. "I honestly don't know if I'll make it. The head cheerleader thinks I'm a freak."

Dad narrowed his eyes then laughed when he realized Annie was serious. "If you're what they're calling freaks these days, then I did all right. And so will you. The squad would be crazy not to have you. Now, go get dressed before that puddle gets any bigger."

Annie put on a black shirt and a denim skirt over black tights, a step up from her usual jeans and T-shirt. Just to look nicer in case she made the cheerleading squad, but the clothes still worked for playing roller derby later that afternoon. It was the final day of the Fresh Meat workshop and Coach Ritter was giving them a test to see if they were ready to play on the team. Annie had no idea what to expect. Even if she didn't pass, she hoped Dad would let her sign up for more practices. Just like living here, she wasn't ready to give up on derby.

Annie and Lexie walked to school together. Lexie was anxious about whether she should add Alice in Wonderland to the bus at Rosie Lee's. "She's a classic but there's no more room for her on the bus and it would make Peter Pan less amusing if he has someone riding on top with him."

"Maybe you can have Alice waiting for the bus?" Annie suggested.

Lexie nodded. "I'll think about that. 'Cause it's not just Alice. I should also have put in Frodo or Bilbo Baggins, I don't know how I forgot a hobbit. And Mom said I have to have Churchill…"

Annie put an arm around her and gave her a squeeze. "It's perfect the way it is. Honestly."

"Thanks. That's the problem with being an artist, you never think it's done. Look how many times Monet had to paint that bridge."

They got to their lockers just in time to hear the principal make the morning announcements over the sound system.

"Good morning, students. First off, I have a very special, confidential envelope that was handed to me by the cheerleading coach. After a gruelling try-out, as some of you know, may I present to you your new Stag cheerleaders…"

Annie took hold of Lexie's hand. This was it. Time to find out whether talent was worth more than Kelsey's opinion.

"Dani Quintana!" Annie and Lexie heard a loud scream from the homeroom next to them.

"Tiffany Lu!"

Annie remembered her; she always had a huge smile.

"Maggie Mae McLaughlin!"

Annie let go of Lexie's hand. She hadn't made it. Kelsey just had too much power. That cheer part was rubbish. And maybe she just wasn't as good a gymnast as she thought.

"And Annie Turner!"

What? No way!

Everyone in the corridor turned around and clapped for her. Annie had to blink a few times to convince herself it was real. She couldn't believe it. She actually got into the squad.

"Congratulations, ladies. Please confirm your acceptance with the captain by Monday. Make us proud," the principal said and turned off the PA system. The bell rang and they headed to their first class.

"This is a first. Me, friends with a cheerleader. I don't know if I can handle it," Lexie said with a grin.

Annie gave her a quick hug. "Remember, first game, you've got to be there. You promised."

Lexie rolled her eyes. "Yeah, all right. Just as long as it doesn't interfere with manga. Or my pottery classes. Or painting my nails."

Annie pushed her playfully. "Oh shut it, you."

"Fine, I'll be there."

"And no drawing me with devil antlers."

"You see how you are? Five minutes as a cheerleader and you already think you're better than the rest of us." Lexie left her in English class and this time Annie rolled her eyes. It was all in good fun, but what if being a cheerleader did change her?

It wasn't impossible. Annie already felt different from the Annie she was back in London. Not worse, just different.

"Hey, I heard the big news. That's so cool you're a cheerleader," Tyler said as he sat down next to Annie in English. Usually he sat towards the back with his friends. And Kelsey. Not that Annie was complaining about the new seating arrangements.

"Thanks." She could feel her face turning red and hoped it wasn't too noticeable.

"It's going to be great having you cheer at my games. Too bad we're playing away tomorrow. But next weekend, you'll be there. It'll be awesome."

Awesome. Yup, having an excuse to stare at Tyler would be awesome. If only she could hold a conversation with him, that might be even more awesome. There he was, sitting right next to her and she could barely speak.

"Yeah." That was it. All she could say. At least she could blame Ms Schwartz for starting the class and cutting their "conversation" short. And attention span. Try as she might, she didn't hear much of what Ms Schwartz said. She was too aware of Tyler right next to her. So close. If he wanted, he could reach out and touch her. At one point she "casually" let her hand drop to her side so it was there if he wanted to hold it. Then she brought it back to the desk immediately, blushing even more. Stupid. He wasn't going to hold her hand. Especially not in the middle of a class. He probably didn't even like her like that. He probably had a girlfriend.

Annie gathered her books quickly at the end of class, hoping to disappear indefinitely.

"Annie, hi." Kelsey sashayed her way over to Annie's desk. She gave her a quick hug that made Annie want to cringe and disinfect her clothes. "I'm SOOO glad you made the squad."

Annie glanced from Tyler, who was beaming, to Kelsey, who was showing enough teeth to envy a crocodile. What was she playing at? "Um, thank you?"

Kelsey linked her arm through Annie's and led her to her next class, and away from Tyler. As they walked down the hallway together, Kelsey gave little waves at the people who turned and looked at them. Any minute Annie expected someone to be sick. She hoped it wouldn't be her.

Kelsey kept up her crocodile smile and added her artificially sweetened voice to it. "As you saw with the try-outs, very few have what it takes to be a cheerleader. I mean really, practices three days a week, sometimes two games per weekend. It's a huge time commitment."

"Yes, I remember," Annie said. The coach had mentioned it during the try-outs. She tried to remove her arm from Kelsey's grip, but Kelsey wasn't finished yet.

"I just want to remind you what an *honour* it is to be a cheerleader. It also means you're popular, so don't do anything that will bring the rest of us down."

Like being mean to the new girl? Although maybe that was better than sickly sweet.

Kelsey finally dropped her arm with a condescending pat and headed to her own seat. "Bye!"

Thanks for the welcome to the team. Good to know I can trust you. Annie sighed and focused on the American History teacher. She couldn't afford to daydream in another class.

Kelsey was right about one thing. Cheerleaders were popular. Every other person, pupil, or teacher who passed Annie in the halls congratulated her on making the squad. Even the cleaner after the last class gave her a thumbs up. It wasn't that Annie wasn't pleased to make the squad, she just didn't have to boast about it to everyone at school. A whole day of Kelsey's fake smiles and everyone congratulating her was too much for Annie. Roller derby practice couldn't come soon enough.

Yesterday her skates had been on the counter, waiting for her when she got to the rink. Today they were nowhere in sight and Jesse was leaning against the rack with his arms crossed.

"You're here," he said, sounding surprised.

Annie gave him a strange look. "Yes, shouldn't I be?"

"I don't know. Derby kind of takes over your life." Jesse shifted his weight from one side to the other.

"Is that a bad thing?"

"I just thought that now you're a cheerleader, you'd stop slumming it with us."

If people weren't congratulating her, they were making snide remarks. Couldn't they see she was still the same person? "Are you kidding? Being here is the highlight of my day."

Jesse relaxed and pulled out her skates. "For real? I figured we'd lost you to the dark side."

Annie pulled her laces up tightly and strapped on her pads. "Well, maybe I'm just what the cheerleading squad needs. A bit of light."

That would go down well; the English girl being a little ray of sunshine. She put on her helmet and joined the rest of the Fresh Meat.

Their warm-up drill today was a game of leapfrog. The girls crouched low and, one at a time, they used each other's backs to push off with their hands to jump over the "frogs". Annie remembered playing leapfrog in the playground when she was younger. Adding skates to the game gave it a whole new meaning. She leaped like she was supposed to over the first few girls, but they were crouched so low, it barely counted. Except the last person. Lauren. When she saw it was Annie's turn, she raised herself to about a metre off the ground and gave Annie a challenging grin. Annie couldn't resist. She knew she could do it.

Annie skated towards her, placed her hands squarely on Lauren's back and leaped over with her legs dangling on either side. She landed on all eight wheels, did a 180-degree turn, and stopped on her toes.

"Awesome." Lauren gave her a high five before they both crouched to the ground for the next frog to leap over them. Looking over at Liz standing a couple of metres away, Annie knew the older girl was impressed.

"All right, peeps." Coach Ritter clapped her hands once

they'd all had a chance to pretend to be leaping frogs. "I hate this part, but it's time for you to show me what you got. Like I said yesterday, this is for safety reasons only. If you've got the skills, you're in the league. While you're waiting your turn, Holly will lead you in some conditioning. Aiko, you're up first."

Holly waved them to the middle of the rink where the refs skated during bouts. By the way Holly avoided being close to her, Annie knew she was still sore about yesterday's knock down.

Holly got them to do leg rotations at the hip, crunches, and girly push-ups on their knees while they waited. Annie shifted from paying attention to the girls on the track to not wanting to know what was going on. She caught Lauren weaving through a minefield of cones and knew she'd definitely make the team.

"Annie, you're next," Coach Ritter called. Annie took a deep breath and skated to her and Liz. "First I want you to skate around three times at the fastest speed you feel comfortable, making sure you don't go out of bounds. After the third lap, stop any way you like. Ready?"

No, but she was going to do it anyway.

Annie got down low, bum sticking out.

Coach blew the whistle and Annie pushed off with her toe to sprint away. She rounded the corners with leg-over-leg crossovers, feeling like she could fly. After the last turn, she dashed to the end as if there were a finish line. With one skate behind, she dragged the wheels to a perfect T-stop. Liz nodded and made some marks on her clipboard.

Next Annie had to jump over a few lines taped on the rink,

side step in both directions, do two kinds of falls, go through the cone minefield as Lauren had, and then skate backwards and stop. Backwards skating still was a bit of a challenge, but at least she was improving. The last thing she had to do was bootie-block one of the other newbies, a girl called Jordan with small black braids and a huge smile. Blocking made Annie the most nervous but also determined to do her best. She managed to keep Jordan from passing her, but only because she was as inexperienced as Annie.

When everyone had completed the test, Holly led all the Fresh Meat in a game of Simon Says while Liz and Coach Ritter compared notes and declared the verdict. Annie could feel her hands sweating as Simon said to skate on one foot. At least they weren't going to make them wait several days like the cheerleading squad. She'd know in a few minutes if she had to appeal to the Skating God or not.

"All righty," Coach Ritter said. "Here are your new roller girls, in no particular order. Lauren, Aiko, Annie—"

Annie let out a scream and didn't hear the rest of the names. Lauren grabbed her in a huge hug and six other girls soon joined them. Even the girls who didn't make it were good sports and congratulated them with pats on their backs. Annie did a little happy dance on her skates that the others quickly tried to copy, resulting in a lot of arms flinging about and one girl on the floor, laughing. Annie couldn't wait to tell her dad, mum, and grandparents about the real good news of the day.

"Good job everyone." Coach Ritter and the older roller girls clapped. "If you didn't make it, come talk to me and I'll give you some feedback on what you need to work on." Handing out a sheet of contact details, she added, "If you made it, practices are here Mondays and Thursdays with bouts on the weekends. See you next week."

What, Mondays and Thursdays? No. No way, not fair. Annie put her head in her hands. Cheerleading practices were Mondays, Tuesdays, and Thursdays. She couldn't be in two places at once. She'd have to choose. But which one?

The one she was better at, or the one she liked better?

Chapter Twelve

"Hey, Annie, check this out." Dad took the cast-iron frying pan off the heat. With a little shake first, he flipped the pancake high into the air. It did three flips before he caught it dead centre back on the pan. "This pancake is a better gymnast than you, Beanie."

Annie raised her eyebrows and reached out for the pan. "Let me have a go."

"No, stop. Intruder. Exterminate!" Dad tried to bar the entry into the kitchen but Annie used her cunning skills to get past the guard.

"Please, please?" Annie looked at her dad with sad, puppy dog eyes.

Dad let out a huge sigh. "I suppose. Nice and easy. Just a flick."

Annie jiggled the pan like Dad had and flipped the pancake in the air. It flipped once and landed half in the pan. The other half broke off and landed on the gas flame. In an instant, Dad grabbed the half pancake with his bare hands and flung it into the sink.

"And that's why, kids, you don't try this at home." Dad pretended to be stern but he was amused. So was Annie. Last time she'd tried to flip a pancake in London, all of it had landed on the floor.

A loud knock came from the front door. Annie opened it to find Lexie standing there with a midriff-baring black and white shirt, high-waisted trousers with braces, and saddle shoes. A white beret perched on top of her unruly hair. "Wow, it smells even better inside."

Dad poked his head out of the kitchen to grin at Lexie, then turned to Annie and got down to business. "Miss Turner, shame on you. Go offer the young lady a seat. I still have to finish up with the flapjacks."

"Hungry?" Annie asked.

Lexie peeked into the kitchen and grinned. "I can eat. If there's enough."

Dad made a humph sound. As if that was even a question.

Annie set the kitchen table for three and gestured to Lexie to sit. She brought out a teapot of hot water, a jug of milk, and the basket with tea bags: black, green, and herbal. She stood back and kept her hands behind her. "And what would you like to compliment your pancakes, miss? Lemon and icing sugar?"

"Butter and maple syrup, if you have it?" Lexie asked, playing along with the game.

"Of course." Annie nodded and turned to Dad. "Order in. Short stack, fat and sweet." In movies, the American cafés always had code names for the food. She wasn't sure if what she said made sense but it sounded good to her.

A few minutes later, Dad set down four plates: three with three pancakes each – one with butter and real maple syrup in little sauce cups, one with lemon slices and dusted with icing sugar, and one with the works. The other plate was piled high with thick bacon.

"Wow," Lexie said to Dad as she took a bite. "If you want another daughter, I can offer myself up for adoption."

"Of course. I can always use another indentured servant for the kitchens." Dad put on an evil voice and twiddled his thumbs mischievously. "I figure twenty years should cover your debt."

Lexie waved a hand at him. "No problem. Though once you get *my* decorating bill…"

Dad narrowed his eyes and growled before the three of them burst out laughing. They clinked their cups of tea and got stuck in. Annie couldn't help but wonder if this was what it was like to have a sister.

"So what's the verdict on cheer-weeding versus derby?" Lexie asked, dipping a piece of bacon into the syrup.

Yup, just like a sister. Bringing up exactly what Annie didn't want to think about. "I don't know. I really wish I could do both."

Lexie agreed. "Not unless you split yourself. Or clone."

Annie pushed her playfully but couldn't help imagining what it'd be like to have a clone. *One of us could go back to London and the other could stay here with Dad.*

"Well, I think you should go for cheerleading," said Dad. "Less chances of getting hurt. String beans aren't as good with bruises."

"Yeah," Annie agreed. To the bruises, not the cheerleading. She still didn't know about that. The pep rally had been so great, and having the whole school watch her perform at the next one would be nerve-wrenchingly brilliant. But she liked the idea of competing more than cheering along the sidelines. And there was no doubt that the girls on the derby team were much nicer. And real.

"Just think," Lexie tried to swing her hair over her shoulder, except it was too wild, so she gave Annie a large cheerleader's smile instead. "If you're a cheerleader, you'll be like one of the most popular girls in like the whole universe!"

Annie swung her own hair, which did swish quite nicely, and held her thumbs and fingers out in a W. "Whatever."

"All righty. Girl talk is always a sign to bail." Dad pushed himself away from the table and stacked the plates on the kitchen counter. "Gotta get some more supplies. I have a challenge for you. See if you can come up with a new recipe– cookie, cake, anything you like – that we can sell at Rosie Lee's."

Annie and Lexie looked at each other. A challenge involving baking? Bring it on.

They put the dishes in the dishwasher and tidied up in the

kitchen. That was one of Dad's few rules and Annie kind of agreed with him: make as big a mess as you need while baking, but never start with a dirty kitchen.

"What do you fancy?" Annie asked as she sipped her Earl Grey tea.

Lexie's eye widened. "How about cupcakes?"

"Ooh, yeah. What kind?"

"Chocolate is always good."

She was right, of course, but Annie wanted to try something different. Something that the people of Liberty Heights had never tasted. She swirled the last bit of the tea in her cup.

That's it!

"What about Earl Grey cupcakes?"

Lexie responded by sniffing one of the tea bags. "Orange?"

"Close," Annie said pulling her hair into a ponytail. "It's called bergamot. I think it's Mediterranean."

"Cool, let's try it. Mind if I plug in some tunes? I brought my MP3 and dock." Lexie didn't wait for an answer. In just a few seconds, Billy Idol's "Rebel Yell" was pumping throughout Rosie Lee's.

"Nice!" Annie gave her a thumbs-up before taking the eggs out of the fridge.

"I'm so glad you dig classic rock. Most kids at school just listen to the mainstream stuff: pop, rap, and hip hop. No imagination."

Annie remembered the annoying pop songs they had to dance to during the cheerleading try-out. If she joined the squad, there'd be no getting away. "Yeah, I've noticed."

Lexie seemed to understand what she was saying. Or not saying. "Cheerleading?"

"They really like their Top 40." Annie started measuring the ingredients. On her seventh birthday Dad had shown her how to make her own cupcakes and she'd never forgotten. The only thing that would be different was to reduce the amount of milk a little to compensate for the extracted tea. She might not be a whizz in the kitchen like Dad, but she knew her way around.

"I still don't get why you want to be a cheerleader. I mean, is it just to be popular like Kelsey?" Lexie asked as she lined the muffin tin with coloured paper cases.

"Kelsey is a you-know-what. I don't want to be anything like her. It's just that…" Annie stopped. She shouldn't have said so much. "I don't want to give up on gymnastics."

Lexie squinted at her. "Really? Gymnastics? That's the only reason?"

"Well," Annie brushed away a stray stand of hair that had come undone from her ponytail. "There is another reason, but it's embarrassing."

"You're dying to show off those insanely long legs in that sickeningly cute uniform?"

The uniform was cute, but no. She took a deep breath. Nicola, Georgie, and Mel back at home knew about him, but that was different because they didn't actually know him. She might as well tell Lexie too. She was her best friend now. "I really fancy Tyler, you know from the football – I mean, soccer – team. I just thought if I was a cheerleader…"

"He'd get to know you better?" Lexie finished for her.

"Pretty stupid, huh?"

Lexie didn't say anything for a bit, and it wasn't just because of the electric mixer. "Look, I don't know him well, him being a junior and all, but I've heard he's kind of a player. I don't want you getting hurt."

"He seems really nice." Annie remembered the talks they'd had: Chelsea Football Club and her accent. He cheered so loudly during her try-out, he had to at least like her as a friend. And then she remembered him flirting with the pretty cheerleaders during the pep rally. "But it doesn't matter. He's way out of my league."

But oh, how great it'd be if they did end up going out. Before taking a penalty shot, he'd look over to the sidelines, catch her eye and signal, "This one's for you, babe," before scoring the goal that would win the game. Then she'd run into his arms—

"Chief, we have a problem," Lexie said to her pretend walkie-talkie. "Anglo girl, fourteen, seems to be suffering from delusions."

Annie pressed pause on her daydream and sighed. Lexie was right. Now was not the time. Tyler fantasies could wait, the cupcakes couldn't. They put the cakes in the oven and started to think about the icing.

"What about lavender? Think that will go well the berga-thingy?" Lexie read the flavours Dad had in stock while Annie sang along with Siouxsie and the Banshees' "Jigsaw Feeling".

"Why not?" Annie swung her ponytail around in headbanging mode then jumped when her phone vibrated in her pocket.

Probably Dad wondering if he'd left his wallet.

No, it was a number Annie didn't recognize.

"Hello?" Annie said as Lexie lowered the music.

"Why haven't you confirmed your spot on the squad? I thought it was very clear that everyone, even you, has to formally accept."

Annie blinked a few times. What? Who? "Is this Kelsey?"

"No, the Easter Bunny," she said so loudly that Lexie heard, making her stick out her teeth, and chest, and hop around like a cheerleading rabbit. Annie had to turn away to keep from bursting out laughing.

"Oh, right. Sorry about that."

"Soooooo? Are you confirming?"

Annie stared out of the lacy curtains Dad still hadn't removed from the kitchen. "Um, can't I let you know on Monday?"

Kelsey made an exasperated sound. "You mean you actually have to think about it? People would kill to be on the squad."

Lexie pointed her fingers into a gun shape and pretended to shoot Annie.

"It's just—" Annie started but Kelsey cut her off.

"Whatevs. Just remember practice is Monday. And please tell me you're not actually listening to that crap I hear. So uncool." And she hung up before Annie could defend the band now playing, the Dead Kennedys.

"Boy, aren't cheerleaders like sooooo sweet and nice?" Lexie asked in the same mocking voice she had used before.

"Shut it." Annie pushed Kelsey out of her mind. If she

became a cheerleader, she'd have to deal with Kelsey *all* the time. How did her minions manage it?

They took out the cupcakes and breathed deeply: the smell was heavenly. When Lexie wasn't looking, Annie pinched off a tiny piece to taste it still warm; Dad always scolded her for doing that even though he did it too. They waited for the cupcakes to cool before adding the icing (which Annie also sneaked a taste of). Here Lexie proved herself an artist. While Annie grabbed a knifeful of icing and slabbed it on top, Lexie sculpted and shaped the icing of each cupcake into a beautiful form. There was no point in Annie helping her. She put the kettle on instead – you couldn't have Earl Grey cakes without Earl Grey tea to compliment them – and tidied up. Once done, the two sat down with a cup of tea and cupcake each. The result? Bliss.

"Ah." Annie put her cup down and started on a second cupcake. "It's a shame good tea is so expensive here. That is the one thing I miss the most."

"What, more than your mom?" Lexie asked.

"No, of course not. It's just…" How could she explain Mum to Lexie without making her sound uncaring? "Mum is very work-driven – some nights she wouldn't even come home until two in the morning."

"That's really late," Lexie said. Annie nodded.

"With me and gymnastics, Mum expected the same: the best. I trained with the top coaches in London. She kept saying that I was going to be the next Nadia Comaneci – she was the first gymnast to score a perfect ten."

"Yeah, I think I've heard of her."

Annie licked the icing slowly off her cupcake. "But when I couldn't compete any more, I think Mum took it worse than I did. If I couldn't be the best gymnast, then I had to be the best something else, but there's nothing else I'm anywhere near as good at. I still don't think she understands me. I love my mum, I really do, but she's nothing like Dad."

Lexie peeled away the paper from her second cupcake. "My mom doesn't get me either. I mean, she's OK with my art, but I know she keeps hoping it'll be something I grow out of."

"At least she's not putting pressure on you."

"Yeah."

"Your mum is really nice. It must be great having her around all the time."

Lexie sighed. "Except when she starts nagging me about not being popular. 'When I was your age, everyone knew me and I always had a boyfriend. I don't understand why you don't.' Of course, she was a cheerleader."

Annie laughed at Lexie's perfect imitation of Mrs Jones. "Maybe we should swap mums like they did on that show on the telly."

"Yes! Can I go to London? Like today?"

Instead of continuing the game, Annie let out the sad truth. "She's probably working. Today, and tomorrow, and every day."

Lexie gave her a big hug, which Annie returned. "Probably because she misses you so much."

"Ta."

Annie jumped at her phone buzzing in her pocket. It was an unknown number.

come down to the skatepark. a bunch of us are chillin.
Jesse.

How did he get my number? Annie wondered. Then she remembered that Coach Ritter had circulated contact details at the end of the last session. Jesse was a non-skating official, so he was on it too. Before Annie could respond, there was another text. This one from Lauren:

Bring your skates and some munchies to the park. Picnic on wheels!

As she was reading it, a text from Liz came in:

Some of us are hanging out at the St Augustine Park on Dalton Street if you want to come.

Annie turned to Lexie. From the expression on her face, Lexie was surprised by Annie's sudden popularity.

"Cheerleading?" Lexie said with a hint of resentment.

"Better. Skate jam at the park. Let's pack up the cupcakes, save a couple for Dad, and head down there."

Lexie was on her feet in an instant. "Now that I can handle. Skater boys are hot."

It took the girls half an hour to walk to the skatepark on the outskirts of town. Annie had never been there before but knew right away she'd be hanging out there again. There were half-pipes and rails, stairs and a flat track. Every person who owned wheels, whether skateboard, roller skates, bicycle, and even one boy in a wheelchair, seemed to be taking advantage of the lasting warm weather to show off their tricks.

Liz, Lauren, and a couple of other girls who played roller derby were practising blocking.

Holly was using the track like a figure skater and showing off her jumps to the roller hockey boys.

Lexie placed herself at the picnic table with her sketchbook to guard the food; Jesse's dog, Sid Vicious, sampled a few of the cupcakes, paper cases and all, as soon as they had put them down.

At Jesse's insistence, Annie climbed the ladder leading up to the half-pipe and laced up her rollerblades. It looked a lot steeper from up above than it did from the ground. Almost a sheer drop. Maybe the half-pipe wasn't such a good idea.

"If you die," Lexie called out. "I'm moving into your house."

Annie stuck her tongue out and then grinned as she buckled the borrowed helmet. "Why wait? We have a spare room."

Before she could think about it any more, Annie went over the edge of the half-pipe.

Oh my god, oh my god, oh my god! She was sure she was going to die! The wind whooshed through her clothes as she went down. A second later she was going up the other side and slowing down big time. No way could she make it to the top. She suddenly realized that once the momentum stopped, she'd go back down – backward! That was so not happening. Just as her speed was about to give out, Annie turned 180 degrees and went down face forward. There were no panicked thoughts this time as she enjoyed the ride. She only made it halfway up the pipe before she turned again. Then one more time up and down before she stopped at the bottom.

She glanced up at Jesse who was watching her from the top of the half-pipe. "I must be mad; I want another go!"

"Sure, but it's my turn now." Jesse launched off the half-pipe as soon as Annie got out of the way. He zoomed down faster than Annie had and when he made it to the top on the other side, he brought his knees to his chest and grabbed the underside of the board with a hand while completing a 360-degree turn mid-air. He landed back on the pipe and returned to the other side where he started. Half the kids at the park cheered, but none louder than Annie. That was brilliant.

Annie spent the rest of the afternoon hanging out with skater boys, roller girls, and anyone else who showed up with wheels, or without. When she got home that night, totally knackered but feeling better than ever, she knew what she had to do. She couldn't debate it any more. There was nothing to debate.

She switched on her computer and wrote an email to Kelsey, copying in the cheerleading coach.

Thanks for selecting me to be a part of the squad. Unfortunately, I'm not going to join at this time as it conflicts with my roller derby training. Good luck with the season ahead.

Best,

Annie

She hit "send" and grinned. Who cared if Kelsey thought she was a punk – Annie was going to be a roller girl!

Chapter Thirteen

Annie walked to her class on Monday feeling great. She couldn't believe how much the cheerleading acceptance had been weighing her down. If she had known how easy it would be to send that email, and how good she'd feel afterwards, she would have done it sooner. Dad was a bit disappointed, but only because he was scared for her. She had explained to him that with Kelsey on the squad, cheerleading was more dangerous than he thought.

And that was before Annie ran into her.

Or rather Kelsey ran into Annie. Kind of, by accident on purpose. Just as Kelsey walked by, she performed the fakest trip possible and practically threw her iced coffee with whipped cream all over Annie.

"Oh dear, I'm *so* sorry," Kelsey said in the phoniest English accent Annie had ever heard while her subordinates pointed and laughed.

Annie wiped the cream from her eyes. Only a bit landed on her face; thankfully it didn't sting. The rest of the drink had gone down her front, quite literally; there were at least two ice cubes nestled in her bra. She shifted her shirt and bra to extract the invasive ice pieces before they did any damage.

"What was that for?" Annie gasped when she finally found her voice.

Kelsey didn't even pretend she didn't know what Annie was talking about. "Because you deserve it."

Annie shook her head to clear it. "Wha—"

"No one, and I mean *no one*, turns down being a cheerleader. Is it because you think you're too good for us? With your stuck-up accent and your punk tastes? Well, you're not."

"No, I nev—" Annie tried to use Lexie's trick of imagining Kelsey with a moustache to lighten things up, but it didn't work.

Kelsey shoved Annie's shoulder like they did on television before a fistfight. "Because let me tell you, you're going to regret turning us down."

"Look, it's—" Annie really wished she knew how to respond. And make Kelsey listen.

"You're such a snob. And you're not that good at gymnastics. Coach only wanted you for affirmative action or something stupid like that."

"That's—" rude, uncalled for, incorrect, and spoken completely silently. If only she had left an ice cube in her bra to chuck at Kelsey.

Someone else was obviously thinking along the same lines. A hand brushed Annie's shoulder and the blob of whipped cream that had been there went flying straight at Kelsey's face.

"Get lost before I kick your pathetic, cheerleading ass!"

Annie blinked a couple of times. The coffee must have distorted her vision. That couldn't be Holly.

It was.

Short, feisty Holly looking like she was ready to pounce on Kelsey and tear her to bits.

"How dare you!" Kelsey screeched as she wiped the cream from her cheek. "I'm going straight to the principal."

"You threw the coffee on me," Annie said. It wasn't the best comeback but at least she'd finally managed to defend herself.

"Do us all a favour and go back to London, and take the leprechaun with you." Kelsey turned away with a mighty swing of her hair, her two subordinates copying her to perfection.

Holly responded by scooping up a handful of ice from the floor and throwing the cubes like darts to the back of their heads. "Oh yeah, come back and say that to my face, you witch."

Several chunks of ice hit their backs, but the girls didn't turn back around, just walked away faster, though Lulu did let out a satisfying, "Ouch!"

Holly mumbled a rude word before grabbing Annie's arm and dragging her to the bathroom. "Let's get you cleaned up."

In the bathroom, Holly grabbed some paper towels and tried to wipe away some of the coffee. Not that it helped. There was still a huge brown stain on Annie's sodden pink shirt.

"That stain's not going anywhere. Not without a washing machine." Holly wet a piece of paper and handed it to Annie to wipe her sticky face and neck.

Annie took it slowly. While part of her worried that Holly was just going to play a meaner trick on her than Kelsey had, the other part wondered if she had misjudged her. Annie let her guard down a bit. "Thanks. You didn't have to stand up for me."

Holly pulled out her make-up bag, not looking at Annie. "Trust me, I know."

"I thought you didn't like me." Annie didn't look at her either as she wet more paper towels.

Holly focused on her reflection as she retouched her eyeliner. "Who says I do? The fact is you're one of us now and no one messes with my roller girls."

Annie smiled. It wasn't exactly a vow of friendship, but she could live with that. "Thanks."

"Yeah, well just don't make me regret it." Holly rolled her newly made-up eyes, but there was a slight smile on her face. Annie relaxed a bit more.

The bathroom door opened and in walked Liz. She took in Annie's stained shirt and Holly's nonchalance and looked worried. "What happened?"

"Kelsey," Annie sighed, still dabbing at her shirt. "She was a bit put out that I chose roller derby over cheerleading."

"Put out?" Holly sniggered. "She went freaking psycho."

True, that was a much better description. "She said no one

turned down cheerleading," Annie said.

"I did." Liz shrugged. "Three years ago, before Kelsey was at the school. It was a different crowd back then with some really nice girls but I decided it wasn't my thing. I wanted to be part of the game, not just cheer from the sides."

That was easy for Liz. She didn't seem like the sort who would take any rubbish from anyone. She was cool and popular just for being who she was.

Annie threw the paper towels in the bin. They hadn't done much good. She'd have to wear a wet and stained shirt for the rest of the day. Or borrow the Hooters shirt from lost and found again. "I just wish I knew why Kelsey hates me so much. I didn't mean to bump into her on my first day in Liberty Heights. It was an accident. Really."

"If I had bumped into her, it wouldn't have been an accident." Holly puckered at her reflection to apply more lipstick.

Liz placed a comforting hand on Annie's shoulder. "She's obviously intimidated by you. The only way she can deal with it is to be nasty."

"Why? I can't even tell her off."

Holly set down her make-up and raised an eyebrow at Annie. "Yeah, we need to work on that."

"You're new and foreign, therefore more interesting. You're also prettier and skinnier than her, which in her mind, counts for everything. And you're by far a better gymnast," Liz said.

Annie narrowed her eyes. Liz was just saying that. There were only a couple of videos of Annie competing on YouTube, and they weren't easy to find. "How do you know?"

Liz grinned. "I saw the try-outs. My little sister wanted to be a cheerleader. She didn't make it. I've tried to get her into derby, but it's not her scene. It'd be awesome if we could put some of your gymnastics moves into derby, but that'd be too dangerous."

Holly finished primping and sighed. "Trust me, I'd give anything to double axel over the pack. Just can't get enough height."

Annie and Liz grinned at each other. Any height Holly lacked she made up for in attitude.

"Thanks, both of you. It's so nice to be part of a team again." Annie looked down at her shirt. It was still wet and stained. If rumours spread as easily as they did at her old school, everyone was going to know what had happened.

Annie bit her lip. She wasn't going to cry. Not in front of Liz and Holly. They'd take back everything and think she wasn't tough enough to be a teammate. She stared at the floor, hoping they didn't notice she was about to break down.

Liz gave her shoulders a squeeze. "Hey, look, I have an extra shirt in my bag. Might be a bit smelly, but at least it's dry."

Annie took a deep breath and gratefully accepted the shirt. She took off hers and put on Liz's. It was a baggy black one but it didn't smell too bad. Annie took another breath. She felt much better now.

The bell rang, causing Annie to jump. She had forgotten they were in the school loos. English next. She glanced at the mirror. Well, she wasn't going to win any beauty contests today but the borrowed shirt at least gave her more confidence. Not enough to pull Tyler into a good snog, but better than having him see her covered in coffee.

Liz held open the door and the three headed out towards class. "Look, forget about Kelsey. You're one of us now. We're a good crowd, you'll see. And we got your back. Trust me, no one messes with a derby girl."

Chapter Fourteen

Annie got to the roller rink, laced up her skates, and sprinted five laps around the rink before she felt human again. The morning's Kelsey coffee catastrophe had been on her mind all day with Kelsey's words ringing in her ears, *"You're such a snob."* Annie was glad to finally have a release.

There were loads more people in the rink than Annie expected. At least forty. There were some girls she recognized from school or the Fresh Meat workshop, but on the whole, they were all new to her.

"Are there really this many on the team?" Annie asked Lauren who was skating next to her.

"This is the whole league, and there are four teams in the league. We play with them, and against them."

"That's a bit odd, isn't it?" Annie asked, though she remembered in the Illinoisies' bout how everyone seemed to be friends rather than rivals.

"That's roller derby for you," Lauren explained. "Teams in a league usually practise together, unless they're too far away."

A brown-haired girl with wide hips and tiny waist skated past them, switched direction and skated backward while talking to them. "Hi, I'm Carmen, a Liberty Belle. Do you know what team you're on?"

Annie and Lauren shook their heads.

"Go find out." Carmen jerked her head to the wall. "Coach Ritter put up the rosters."

Annie and Lauren looked at each other and raced towards the wall. Annie got there a second before Lauren and did a perfect tomahawk stop in front of the list. She found her name on the third list, along with Lauren's and about eleven others. They were Liberty Belles too, still coached by Coach Ritter, and Liz was their captain. Brilliant. Holly was also a Belle. Good. Even though Annie and Holly were cool now, she wouldn't have liked competing against her; the bruise on her thigh from their crash last week was still the size of Wales.

Lauren linked her arm through Annie's and stood tall. Even so, she only reached just above Annie's shoulder. "Now you can officially be my wife."

Annie shook her head and smiled. "Pardon?"

Lauren let go of her but kept a mischievous gleam in her eye. "Derby wives. Good friends that have each other's backs and are there for the other in a jam. Whatcha think?"

Why not? Lauren was a great roller girl and Annie really liked hanging out with her. Besides, it was all in good fun. "I think I better tell my parents I've got hitched."

Lauren laughed and punched her on the shoulder.

The Prairie Girls' coach, Shanti Morningstar, called everyone to the middle. Her thick blonde dreadlocks bouncing, she explained the first drill.

"Welcome everyone. Today we're playing a variation on tag called Jaws. We're starting with one shark and the rest of you are fish. If the shark catches you, you become a shark too and need to skate over here and put on a helmet panty so the fish can avoid you. If you skate out of bounds, as a fish or shark, you're out of the game. Newbies, really keep an eye out. It's your responsibility not to get tagged *and* avoid crashing into anyone. Sharmila, you wanted to be the first shark."

A gorgeous girl with brown skin, green eyes and black hair glided more than skated to the middle of the rink and beamed. With her perfect glittering make-up, designer skirt, and workout shirt, Annie would have thought she was a Bollywood star not a roller girl. She hadn't been part of the Fresh Meat so that must mean she'd been in the league for a while. Annie got a feeling that in this girl's case, looks were deceiving.

She was right. As soon as the whistle blew, Sharmila proved that being gorgeous didn't mean she wasn't tough. Within ten seconds, she had tagged three people. Now with four sharks on the loose, and about forty people trying to get away, Annie really had to concentrate. There were so many girls, skating in every different direction. Twice she almost got forced out of bounds, but just managed turn sharply to avoid getting tagged. Every once in a while a whistle would blow and a coach would signal a girl out of the game for going out of bounds.

Annie spotted Carmen coming up behind her, and twisted away across the rink. Her head whipped around in every direction, keeping a look out for skaters wearing helmet covers. Carmen whizzed past, switched targets, and pelted across to a girl with short black pigtails.

The fish were dwindling and the sharks were gaining force. Half of the girls, including Lauren and Liz, had been sent off for going out of bounds. There were only about five fish left in the entire sea. And Holly the Shark locked her eyes on a British delicacy. Annie stared at Holly for a second before a small grin crept over her face. She knew Holly was competitive, but Holly probably didn't know that she was as well. At the same instant Holly lunged at her, Annie sprinted off. She darted from one end to the other, weaving around other sharks who were after the remaining fish, but there was no shaking off Holly.

Annie felt a hand brush across her arm. She'd been caught. Holly wore a smug smile but nodded to indicate she was impressed with Annie's performance.

The rest of the fish were caught before Annie had a chance to put on her helmet cover.

"Great work, everyone." Coach Ritter and the other coaches clapped. "Now let's work with packs of blockers, passing them

147

and going through. Four separate packs on each side of the rink. Carmen, Bea, Lauren, and Annie form a wall over here, Holly you're jammer."

The four got together and Carmen took charge. "Have you two been part of the pack yet?"

Annie and Lauren shook their heads. Annie gulped. She was not looking forward to this.

Carmen continued while slipping on a helmet cover with a broad stripe. "I'll pivot, which means I set the pace and call orders. You three stay with me. If we spread apart, she can pass us easily. If we're a solid wall, we can hold her back."

Coach Morningstar blew her whistle. Lauren squatted down to her derby stance and looked so intimidating there was no way any jammer would try getting past her. Annie tried to copy Lauren and knew the result was more like a rabbit glaring at headlights than intimidation.

The whistle blew again and Holly charged towards them. In just a matter of seconds, Annie had to focus on skating with the pack and keeping Holly from scoring. She couldn't imagine what it'd be like with five more players on the track. How could she possibly play offence and defence at the same time?

Annie, holding onto Lauren's hips, did what Carmen had suggested to block Holly. It didn't work. Holly passed them as if they weren't even blocking her way. And just to prove her point, she cut through the middle of the rink, got behind, and passed them again without even trying.

"Newbie," Carmen called to Annie. "Don't be afraid to block

her. Your job is to not let her get by."

Annie nodded. She understood what she needed to do though she wasn't really sure she could put it in action.

"It's OK, wifey." Lauren punched her on the shoulder. "Just got to work on being more solid."

Easy for her to say. Lauren was about as solid as they got. Annie hadn't seen her get knocked over once.

She tried blocking a few more times with different people as jammers. The plus side was that she was getting better; she actually blocked a couple of girls and when they broke through, it wasn't because of her. The downside was that they were newbies as well.

When it was her turn as jammer, she was determined to prove her worth. Crouched low, she pushed off and ran on her toe stops as soon as her whistle blew. She reached the pack in an instant but couldn't get through. Derby wife or not, Lauren wasn't going to make it easy for her. And Holly might only be forty-five kilos, but she was super quick and in the way whenever Annie tried to pass. She only just managed to get past another newbie when the whistle blew, signalling that the two minutes were up.

"Good job, peeps. Take five, grab a breather," Coach Ritter called out and motioned to Annie come towards her. Oh dear lord. She was being kicked off. Coach realized she had made a mistake and Annie didn't really have the skills to play.

"Go get your skates checked out, Annie. I think your wheel bearings might need cleaning." Coach Ritter pointed to Jesse behind the skate rental booth. Annie let out a sigh of relief. She wasn't being booted off. Yet.

She took off her skates and handed them to Jesse to clean up. He whistled when he gave a wheel a test spin. "Yup, they need some juice for sure. So, have you come up with a cool derby name?"

Annie shook her head. "No, I haven't thought about it really. Have you got any ideas?"

His face lit up as he cleaned the skates. "Loads: I-Tarzan U-pain, Lady Gagya, Buffy the Tramp Slayer, Sin Bin McQuinn. If you were Lexie, you could be Lex Lethal."

Not bad, though Annie knew her best friend well enough that if she were a roller girl, her name would be something along the lines of Freaka Kahlo. "What would your name be, if you played?" Annie asked.

Jesse didn't even pause to think about it. "Death Vader. It's my ref name."

That was a good one.

"I guess I want something I can relate to. That says who I am." Annie pulled out her hairband to redo her ponytail.

"What about Hairy Slaughter?"

Annie pushed him lightly on the arm. "I don't have that much hair."

In response, Jesse tried to blow his black fringe out of his blue eyes before handing back her skates. Annie took hold of her skates slowly. He really had gorgeous eyes. With his hair covering his face most of the time, his eyes were easy to overlook.

"All right peeps, let's get back to work," Coach Ritter called them back for practice.

Annie laced up quickly and rejoined everyone on the rink. The difference in her skates was unbelievable. Like she could turn just by thinking about it. Now if that would only help her blocking, she'd be in good shape.

Over the sound system came the Sex Pistols' song, "Anarchy in the UK".

Great song, Jesse. Annie sang the lyrics in her head when it hit her. Anarchy. Anne R. Key.

She couldn't help it. Even though the coaches had called them over to the middle, she had to tell him first. Jesse saw her racing to him and leaned over the barrier.

"Skates too slick?" he asked.

Annie shook her head with a huge smile and pointed to the speakers. "That's me. That's my derby name. Anne R. Key!"

"Sweet! That's definitely you." He gave her a high five and cranked the volume a bit higher.

Annie spun around and soared back to group. Of course Jesse would think it was brilliant. He'd named his mutt Sid Vicious.

"Let's hold a scrimmage. Liberty Belles versus Prairie Girls and High Rollers versus Derby Dolls. Each set of teams will skate one jam on, one jam off. Jesse, if you're free, we could use you as a jam ref." One of the coaches waved his clipboard. Jesse nodded. In less than a minute he'd hopped over the barrier in battered quad skates, a whistle swinging around his neck.

Annie watched the first couple of jams from the bench. At the Illinoisies' bout she hadn't fully appreciated how chaotic it all was. It was impossible to watch what everyone was doing. Girls went every which way and the coach refs kept sending players to the penalty box for things Annie couldn't figure out. When Coach Ritter put her out as a blocker it dawned on Annie that she was finally going to play roller derby, even if it was just a scrimmage. Wicked!

She huddled next to Lauren. That had to work. No one could get by Lauren.

Good thought, but not very realistic.

The whistle blew and the jammers sprinted towards the pack. Annie looked over her left shoulder, over her right, over her left again. The Prairie Girl jammer, LaTicia, was right at her side, trying to barge her way through. But Lauren was also at Annie's side and she wasn't budging. LaTicia darted to Annie's other side. One of the opposing blockers got in Annie's way, allowing LaTicia to slip right through. Jesse blew his whistle twice to indicate LaTicia was the lead jammer and followed her from the middle of the rink with his arms in an L-shape. Holly got through the pack seconds later.

"Newbie," Carmen shouted to Annie. "You can block other players too. Not just the jammer."

"And don't forget to move. You're on skates, use them," Liz added.

Annie crouched low and looked over her shoulder. LaTicia was seconds away. Carmen and Lauren huddled around Annie. She felt the jammer push against her and she pushed back. LaTicia tried the other side and Annie didn't let her through that way either. She knew it was because her teammates were glued to her side but Annie was glad she managed a good block. The Prairie Girls' pivot came to rescue LaTicia. Annie gathered herself up for a big bootie-block swing at the pivot.

And landed on her hands and knees.

That wasn't nearly as bad as I thought it'd be.

She pushed herself up and returned quickly to the pack. Just because LaTicia had passed her didn't mean she had to give up. Moments later, Annie bootie-blocked LaTicia out of bounds before she could score more points. LaTicia quickly called off the jam. When Jesse blew the whistle, Annie welcomed the quick break while the High Rollers and Derby Dolls took the track. Her hair was plastered with sweat underneath the helmet. That was much more tiring than she had expected.

But so much fun!

In their next jam, Lauren was put as jammer.

"Who's got my panty?" Lauren shouted with a grin before someone threw her the starred helmet cover that identified her as a jammer.

As Annie watched Lauren slip the panty over her helmet, she felt a twinge of jealousy. Lauren was great, Annie had agreed to be her derby wife after all, but they had started at the same time. Annie knew she was the better skater and wondered when it would be her turn to have a go as a jammer.

Coach Ritter seemed to know what she was thinking. "You got to learn to block before you can be a jammer. Keep working on it."

Annie did. She was put in as a blocker for a few more jams. Jammers still sneaked right by her but at least she could delay them now. In one brilliant jam, Annie, Sharmila, and two other girls managed to hold off the jammer while Holly almost danced on her toe stops to get in front and become the lead.

Soon, Annie thought. *Soon, I'll be a jammer too.*

She focused on that and it helped with her blocking. It didn't scare her so much any more. It helped that she also had a motive.

"Annie, good improvement." Coach Ritter clapped as they skated off to let the other two teams play. "If you're not too tired, why don't you try being jammer next jam."

Holly threw her the helmet panty. "Look, the secret isn't to barge your way through. It's to find opportunities, even the smallest, and grab them."

Annie gave her a smile. "Thanks."

Holly rolled her eyes as if to say whatever, but then smiled back.

Annie got ready ten metres behind the pack and was out running as soon as she heard the sound of the second whistle. She headed straight for the centre of the pack. If she could just duck between them... Wait, was there a gap to the side? Yes! She squeezed through and she was past the pack. Jesse had his arms in an L-shape and was grinning so much the whistle slipped out of his mouth. That meant she was the lead jammer!

With a great burst, Annie raced around the track. The other jammer, she knew, was not far behind. If she could only make it through the pack again, she could call off the jam before the other jammer scored points.

When Annie had nearly reached the pack, Carmen held out her arm. Annie knew what to do – she'd seen the Illinoisies do it. With a mighty swing, Carmen whipped her to the front of the pack. Or what had been the front. In a flash, the Prairie Girls' pivot was in front, breaking Annie's momentum. With no time to change direction, Annie crashed smack into the pivot. The two hit the floor hard, along with Carmen and two others whose limbs could be seen flailing about. It was a pile-up.

And it was all Annie's fault.

Annie scrambled back to her feet and called off the jam before the other jammer could score more points, but it had been a total disaster. She knew she wouldn't be picked as jammer anytime soon.

And here she'd been thinking that she was finally good at something again.

Chapter Fifteen

Unsurprisingly, Coach Ritter didn't play Annie as jammer again at the next practice, but she made sure Annie got a good amount of time blocking.

"You got to learn to block before you can be a jammer." Coach Ritter's words played like a mantra in Annie's head. If that's what it took, she was going to do it. The thrill of breaking through the pack and skating around the rink at top speed was something she hadn't felt since she retired from the uneven bars. She got Lauren to stay with her an extra half an hour after practice on Thursday to work on the blocking.

"I really think you're getting the hang of it." Lauren unclipped her helmet after they had finally made it around the rink with Annie blocking Lauren and not letting her pass.

"Thanks for the help. I couldn't have done it without you." Annie took off her own helmet and crumpled onto the bench.

"No sweat." Lauren wiped her drenched forehead and laughed. "That's what derby wives are for."

"Do you think I'll get a chance to play jammer on Saturday?" Annie asked. Saturday, their first bout. Just thinking about it terrified her.

Lauren shrugged. "Coach seems really fair. If she thinks you can to do it, she'll let you."

Annie sighed. She'd been skating everywhere around town to build up her endurance and thought she'd done better today at blocking than last practice, but Coach hadn't seemed to notice. On the other hand, she hadn't criticized Annie's blocking so maybe that was a good sign.

"Hey, I just remembered. What's your playing number going to be?" Lauren peeled off the zebra-patterned duct tape securing her kneepads.

Annie squinted. She hadn't thought of a number. "Won't Coach just give me a random number no one else has?"

"Not in derby. You can be creative and can use letters, symbols, whatever. Liz's number is '1000rpm', Holly is '97lbs', lucky duck. There's a woman in the adult league who's '−0' and another who's '50ish'. She's actually fifty-six years old and still playing derby!"

If Annie were a roller girl in her fifties, she'd boast about it too. "What's yours?"

Lauren grinned, clearly feeling proud of herself. "10^{24}."

"That's a massive number," Annie said. "Why did you pick it?"

"It's a yottabyte. Makes megabytes and gigabytes on computers look like babies, an inside computer-nerd joke. I love it. That's the thing with derby numbers. They should mean something to you."

If that was the case, Annie needed to give her number more thought. She'd always liked the number 96 – it was the same upside down and it was the year her parents got married – but that seemed a bit dull after "50ish".

Lauren had finished packing up all her things.

Annie noticed a hoodie on top of the lockers and brought it down. "Is this yours too?"

"Yeah, thanks. I didn't see it and forgot I threw it up there." Lauren pulled on the black hoodie covered in brown and white dog hair.

Annie shrugged. "That's what derby wives are for. At least tall ones."

"I like tall girls. What can I say, I've got good taste." Lauren punched Annie's shoulder and headed outside. "See ya."

Annie waved and gathered up the last of her things. People didn't often compliment her on her height. It was nice. She had got so used to everyone saying how unfortunate her height was for gymnastics that she never really thought about it as an asset. She stood up straight and pulled her shoulders back. Why shouldn't she feel proud of being five foot eleven and a half? It was just a number.

Number!

With a new burst of energy, Annie skated home at top speed. She knew exactly what her derby number would be.

Saturday arrived suddenly. But before Annie's first bout that evening was an event just as exciting: Rosie Lee's grand opening. Annie got to the café at eight in the morning.

Everything looked perfect. Dad had finally broken down and got a professional team to put in a new floor over the stubborn paint stain and gnarly raw bits left from where the booths had been. The result was a gleaming black and white chequered floor. The tables and chairs looked inviting, everything was spotless, and Lexie's mural was eye-catching enough to attract attention from people passing by outside.

And that was all nothing compared to the gorgeous displays of scones, croissants, cupcakes, muffins, tarts, cakes, and cookies (they weren't British, but there were no good cookies in town – both Annie and Dad had checked).

Dad had been baking since four in the morning. He was just finishing the sandwiches when Annie got there.

"Place looks great, Dad. I'm really proud of you."

Dad leaned over and kissed her on top of her head. "Same here, Beanie."

Annie checked the coffee, normal and decaf. Done. Hot water tap. On.

"Are you ready?" Annie asked, slapping her thighs like a drum roll. Dad tied on a clean apron and took a deep breath before nodding.

With a flamboyant gesture, Annie flipped the sign from "Closed" to "Open".

"So what can I do?" She let out her breath and smoothed out invisible creases on the tablecloths.

"Glad you asked," Dad said. "I printed some coupons I want you to hand out. Free coffee or tea with every pastry or sandwich. Watcha think?"

Annie held an invisible microphone to her mouth and put on a deep movie-voiceover accent. "David Turner was just a small town boy until the day his baking changed life in Liberty Heights forever."

Dad bowed and blew kisses at the imaginary crowd. "I'd like to thank everyone who made this moment possible, especially my gods Dionysus and Edesia. And I suppose my daughter too, if I must."

Annie threw a packet of sugar at him. "Cheeky!"

Dad laughed and pulled her into a tight hug. "You're the best, Beanie."

"You're OK too, I guess," Annie teased before pulling away. "Shall I grab my rollerblades, that way I can zoom all over town passing out the coupons?"

Dad ducked back into the kitchen and wiped down the clean counter. "Ah, well, I was hoping you'd do me another favour."

"Why aren't you looking at me? Is it something horrid?"

Annie crossed her arms.

Dad faffed about adjusting the wrapping on one of his sandwiches. "Not horrid. I thought it'd be fun. See, since it's a British-style café, I got you something to wear while you hand out the coupons."

"OK," Annie said, sounding wary. "But it better not be a Union Jack dress."

Dad didn't answer. Instead he pulled out something covered in dry-cleaning plastic. "They didn't have many options at the costume store. It was either this or James Bond."

It couldn't be too bad if 007 was the other option. Wrong. The dress was frumpy with a matching handbag and came with a short curly grey wig and crown. An image she'd seen her whole life came to mind.

"The Queen? You want me to dress like the Queen?" Bond would have been a much better choice.

Dad started rushing around, searching for something to do. "I looked for a Kate Middleton-type dress but there wasn't anything that would let people know who you were without explaining it."

Annie didn't think many people here would know she was the Queen either. "Do I have to wear this? It's just that it's a bit embarrassing."

Dad forced a smile. "No, if you don't want to that's OK. I just thought it'd be fun and help bring attention to the café."

Put that way, Annie couldn't say no. "All right, then. But I'm still wearing my rollerblades."

The bells attached to the front door jingled and an old woman with blue hair poked her head in. "The sign says you're open."

"That we are." Dad darted over and opened the door the rest of the way for his first customer. By the time Annie left dressed like Queen Elizabeth II – on rollerblades – there were three more people in the café and Dad already knew them all by name.

Everyone outside who passed by turned to glance at Annie; it wasn't everyday a bootie-blocking queen whirled around Liberty Heights. She hated all the stares, but kept reminding herself it was for Dad as she smiled and handed out coupons.

"Are you a real queen?" asked a little girl around five years old.

Annie didn't know how to answer that. She didn't want to lie but she didn't want to be the one to tell the little girl that people in costumes weren't always real. She went for a different approach: changing the subject. "What's your name?"

The girl looked at her mother who nodded approval before answering. "Clara."

Annie crouched on her skates to get to her level. "Clara, that's pretty. Would you like to try on my crown?"

The little girl nodded her head enthusiastically. Annie placed the crown on her hair and smiled as the girl's mother took a picture.

"What do you say, Clara?" her mother urged when Annie placed the crown back on her wig.

"Thank you, your majesty," Clara said, curtseying.

Annie smiled and skated off. OK, maybe the outfit wasn't

that bad. She worked out who were the best people to approach with coupons, and who to avoid. Businessy types crossed to the other side of the street when they saw her coming. People on phones just threw the coupon away in the bin without looking at it. Mothers with four young kids heading to the barbershop also didn't need a distraction. But retired men on benches, people strolling leisurely, and anybody else who had the time for a ten second chat about Rosie Lee's got a coupon.

Heading back to the café to replenish her coupons, Annie found things really buzzing. Dad was running from one place to the other with a huge grin on his face, barely keeping up with everything that needed doing. Annie jumped in to brew a new pot of coffee, empty the dishwasher, and put six cupcakes in a white bakery box for Clara and her mother.

"I hope you know you'll have to wear that costume again, or Clara here will be very sad." The mother winked and Clara waved until they turned the corner. Annie waved back but inside she was wincing. As much as she hated disappointing Clara, she hoped she never had to see the costume again.

She grabbed some more coupons and spotted Lexie and her parents sitting at a table with a proper cream tea: English breakfast tea served with scones, strawberry jam, sliced strawberries, and fresh clotted cream, which Dad had to make himself. Next to them was a box that Annie imagined held a sample of some other treats. On the house, of course.

"Hey, Annie, great look." Lexie grinned, but knowing Lexie's taste in fashion (today, even though it was getting chilly, she was in a Hawaiian-print dress with a flower in her hair), Annie couldn't tell if she was being sarcastic or serious. "Though the footwear is a bit off."

Right, sarcasm it was. "Next time *you* wear the dress, and I'll keep the skates."

Lexie's eyes lit up. "Bring it."

Dad came over to the table during a quick pause of the madness. "Thanks for coming, guys. Always a pleasure to have you here. Everyone has been asking me about the mural, Lexie. Fantastic work. You have a very talented daughter."

"Thanks," the three Joneses said. Mrs Jones added, "And Annie is such a joy as well."

Annie blushed while Dad gave a cocky Han Solo-type smile. "I know."

The doorbells jingled and Dad ran off to tend to the next customers.

"I better go too. Dad printed five hundred coupons that I have to hand out," Annie said.

Mrs Jones, who only reached Annie's chest with Annie's added skate height, wrapped her in a tight hug. Instead of embarrassing her, the hug made Annie miss Mum. It had been a long time since she'd had a hug from her.

"See you later tonight?" Annie asked Lexie, trying to distract herself from how she felt.

"Wouldn't miss it." Lexie pulled a large bag out from under the table and hugged Annie too. "Here, don't open it until you get to the rink."

"Thanks." Annie grinned and put it out of the way in the kitchen before skating off with more coupons.

Like some horrid déjà vu, Annie turned the corner and encountered her worst nightmare. She didn't jump over a dog and crash into someone's yogurt, but it was just as bad. There, right in front of her, surrounded by friends, was Kelsey. With Tyler at her side.

Annie quickly changed direction, but wasn't quick enough.

"Annie," Tyler called.

Face glowing, wig and crown suddenly feeling very heavy, Annie slowly turned back around. With a deep breath, she skated towards them and gave Tyler a coupon.

"'British-style café,'" Tyler read from the paper in his hand. "I thought British food was kind of gross."

He was teasing, she knew that, but it still stung a bit. Even if Dad wasn't British. "We've come a long way since the olden days."

"Not far enough," said Kelsey, jutting out a hip. "Or they would have taught you something about fashion."

"Hey lay off, Kels," Tyler defended her. "Annie's just wearing that for advertisement, right?" A panicked look suddenly crossed his face, as if he thought that maybe Annie really was wearing the costume because she liked it.

"Right," she agreed, though she would have agreed with Tyler about anything at that moment. He had stood up for her! "Hope to see you around."

She held up her coupons in a wave and started to skate away.

"Wait," Kelsey said. "Don't I get one?"

Annie did a T-stop and glanced from her coupons to Kelsey. "I wouldn't have thought you needed any cakes, Kelsey, seeing as you're so sweet already." Her voice was dripping with sarcasm.

Everyone, except Kelsey, laughed at Annie's remark as she skated away. She shouldn't have stooped to Kelsey's level, but it certainly felt good finally getting one up on her.

Annie helped out for most of the afternoon in the busy café. Towards the end of the day, when things got quieter, she skated around the downtown again to hand out more coupons. Just before five o'clock, Annie returned to Rosie Lee's, coupons all gone. There was one customer left, enjoying late afternoon treacle tart and tea, and an energetic chat with Dad about being an American in London. Annie wriggled out of her queen garb, grateful that the costume shop hadn't included a corset, and helped herself to one of the leftover sandwiches. By the time she'd finished, the last customer was gone, as were the remaining slices of the tart.

"Good day, yeah?" Annie asked as she poured out the coffee and cleaned the containers.

Dad's eyes shone as he changed the sign from "Open" to "Closed". "The best. Ran out of the lemon and mascarpone scones by noon. The anise shortbread disappeared after I gave away some samples. And that last guy, Simon, took the rest of the treacle tart home to his family and wants me to make the cake for his six year old's birthday tea party."

"That's brilliant. I'm really glad."

A car outside honked. Annie looked at the clock and knew it was time.

"That's Liz. She's taking me to the bout. You're coming, right?"

They looked around the empty café. There was so much cleaning to do – and the display case was almost empty.

Dad sighed. "I don't know, Beanie. There's a lot I have to do before tomorrow. But I'll try."

Annie gave him a hug before grabbing Lexie's surprise bag and running out to the car. Her stomach was in knots and she knew it was more than just nerves. She really hoped Dad would make it; he had been to every single one of her gymnastics meets. It was Mum, never Dad, who always had to work late.

One workaholic parent was bad enough. She didn't want to think what it'd be like to have two.

Chapter Sixteen

In the locker room, a black and red T-shirt came flying towards Annie's head. She caught it with one hand. Straightening it out, she couldn't stop staring at it. The front had Lady Liberty in derby gear with a tough scowl on her face but the back was the best:

Anne R. Key. 5'11" ½.

Perfect.

She put it on along with a pair of fishnets she and Lexie had bought and her lucky silver gymnastics shorts. Lauren wrote "5'11"½" on Annie's arms using a marker pen and Annie wrote Lauren's number on hers. Pads and skates on. Mouth guard and helmet at hand. She was ready to go.

"Annie, where are you going?" Sharmila said.

"Just having a look at the crowd," she said, but Sharmila shook her head and pointed back at the bench.

"Not without your face." Sharmila sat in front of her and began applying make-up. "I'm going for fierce sparkle with you."

Annie didn't know how to argue, and wasn't sure she wanted to. Girls in gymnastics always plastered on the make-up. It was a bit like preparing for battle by applying war paint. Holly looked like a Hollywood starlet with 1930s make-up and freshly dyed flame-red hair. Liz had a green painted mask that resembled a butterfly. Lauren was done up with two black streaks under her eyes like an American football player – she had flat out refused anything that looked remotely girly, though her mid-thigh shorts were hot pink.

When Sharmila handed Annie a mirror she couldn't believe it was her. She wouldn't have thought to give herself that look, but the result was amazing: nastily cool scars on one side and stars on the other with almost as much glitter as Sharmila herself.

"All right, peeps." Coach Ritter came in with a clipboard and her long auburn hair pulled into two low pigtails. "I know we were bottom of the league last year, but we've got a killer team now, so let's show them what we got. Warm up's in two minutes."

Annie stood up and remembered Lexie's surprise package. She took a quick peek to see what it was. Good thing she did. Lexie had got her a helmet and decorated it with a Warhol-esque portrait of Annie. It was utterly amazing.

Lauren leaned over. "Wow. Did you paint that yourself?"

Annie shook her head as she strapped it on. "My best friend

Lexie is a brilliant artist."

"I'll say."

The team skated onto the rink to warm up. There weren't very many people there and Annie quickly found Lexie waving a banner with old-fashioned house keys that said "Total Anne R. Key!"

Annie waved, pointed to her helmet, and shouted, "It's brilliant. Cheers."

Lexie responded by waving her banner more.

Annie kept skating around. She saw Jesse by the sound system and a few kids she recognized from school. But no Dad.

He'll come. He's never let me down. But Annie couldn't help but worry that this would be the first time.

Liz got them to do some stretches before gathering them around by the sidelines. "Everyone looks great. Remember that blocking we've been working on, but most of all don't forget to have fun."

They cheered and sat on the benches.

"Good evening, roller derby fans," Jesse said into the loudspeaker. "Tonight's bout is between the Liberty Belles..." Annie's team all cheered. "...and the Derby Dolls!"

Maybe it was her imagination but there seemed to be a considerably louder cheer from their team and supporters. If Dad were here, he'd put cheerleaders to shame with his booming voice.

"She might only be ninety-seven pounds but watch out for Holly Terr-rror!" Jesse introduced her. Holly skated around the rink backward and did a jump like figure skaters on television, landing on one skate.

"Feel the love as Sharmila the Hun sends out those X0X0s!" Sharmila didn't skate around, but stood blowing kisses at the crowd and looking gorgeous as always.

"And here comes your Liberty Belle captain, going at one thousands revs per minute, make way for ElizaDEATH!" Liz skated around the track then dropped to one knee and spun around.

As Lauren skated onto the track, her face beaming, Jesse announced, "Time to call the cops, because Lauren Disorder – number ten to the power of twenty-four – is in the house!"

It was Annie's turn next.

"One of Liberty Belles' newest editions, from London, England, we have number five foot eleven and a half, Anne R. Key!"

As Jesse introduced the rest of the girls, Annie skated around the track at top speed, stopped, and slid into the splits. As she swung her leg around, she saw the look of surprise, and pain, on several people's faces.

The bout started with Liz as pivot to set the pace and call the plays, three more blockers called Cookie, Bea, and Tashi, and Holly as the jammer. The first whistle blew and the blockers bundled up, moving in the directions dictated by their pivots. When the second whistle went off Holly dodged a side block from the other jammer as she sprinted towards the pack. As they rounded the first corner, away from the benches, Annie had a hard time watching everything at once. There was so much going on it looked like just a horde of girls on the track. One of the refs sent Hell's Angelica from the other team to the penalty box for elbowing, and Holly sneaked through the gap.

"Holly Terror, first out of the pack, and she's your lead jaaa-mmer!" Jesse announced while the crowd cheered. Holly switched to backwards skating and blew kisses towards the crowd as she performed beautiful backwards crossovers. She switched to forwards skating as the other jammer started to catch up. Hell's Angelica came back from the box and the other team had a full number of players in their jam again. With some quick dodging, Holly squeezed through a tiny slot to pass the pack again. From the sideline Coach Ritter frantically tapped her arms against her hips. Holly responded to the coach's signal and flapped her own arms to call off the jam.

Annie looked at the score. 4-1 in the Liberty Belles' favour.

Sharmila was the next jammer with Liz still as pivot. They were joined by Lauren, Carmen, and a girl that was in Annie's French class. Carmen and a Derby Doll got sent to the box briefly during that jam. They served their time in the box just as the jam was called off so they didn't have to carry their time over to the next jam. Derby Dolls' jammer, Polly Socket, scored three points while Sharmila scored two.

"Natalia jammer. Holly pivot. Lauren, Tashi, Annie, get in there," Coach Ritter called out.

Annie took in a sharp breath and skated out onto the rink. This was it.

"Princess," Holly said to Annie. "Watch those gaps."

Annie nodded. She could do this. Just like practice. She crouched down feeling out of place next to Holly who was half her size, and Lauren who was bigger than her.

The second whistle blew and she looked over her shoulder. The other team's jammer, Mo Jo, was heading her way. Annie remembered her from league practices: Mo liked to sneak by on the outside. Except Lauren had the outside covered and there was no getting by her as she knocked Mo to her knees.

Annie kept her eye on Mo, as she quickly got back on her feet. Lauren shifted to the inside to help Natalia get through. Mo came up behind, saw Lauren, and veered quickly to Annie's right. Annie knew what she was going to do and was ready for her. With a mighty swing, Annie bootie-blocked Mo and sent her flying out of bounds.

Now that was fun! All this time Annie had been focusing on being jammer, she hadn't realized how great blocking was. Lauren showed off her leopard-print mouth guard as she grinned. Together they blocked the Derby Dolls' blockers, letting Natalia pass and score some points.

Annie stayed on the rink for the next jam, this time with Liz back as pivot and Holly as jammer. Tashi had been sent to the box in the jam before so they were down one player. Annie was pleased that Coach trusted her enough to keep her in.

"As Holly Terror comes around, ElizaDEATH, Cookie Crumbles, and Anne R. Key form an impenetrable wall," Jesse spoke fast trying to keep up with all the action. "One player short, they're not letting Slam I. Am sneak by. ElizaDEATH blocks the Dolls' pivot Polly Socket, giving Holly Terror that break to become your lead jammer! Slam I. Am is still trying to find her way through. She tries to get by Anne R. Key, but the newbie is not having it and gives the jammer a mighty block. Holly Terror comes back around. If she passes the whole pack including the other team's jammer, that's a grand slam. Can she do it? Yes! Hey, Slam I. Am, guess what? You've just been grand slaaaammed!"

The Liberty Belles got their player back from the box, who was replaced by Bea, and they played the full two minutes of the jam with Holly racking up fourteen points. Panting as she came off the rink, Annie sat down for her break. The team was playing well, but so were the Derby Dolls, and the scores stayed pretty close. With each jam she played, Annie felt more confident with blocking. When the buzzer sounded for half-time they were only lagging by two points. In derby scores, that was nothing.

Coach Ritter gathered them around in the locker room. "You're doing great, peeps. Everyone's blocking has been right on the money and they're getting worried, I know it. Keep up the great defence but now we have to up the offence. Help your jammer and let's show them Liberty Belles aren't going to be at the bottom of the league this year!"

They all cheered before settling down to fix equipment and make-up. Annie went to the bathroom, drank water, made sure her pads were still secure, and skated back out five minutes before the half-time ended.

She motioned to Lexie to come over to the barrier and gave her a huge hug. "Thanks for the helmet. It's fantastic! Everyone in the locker room was dead jealous. I know Sharmila and Bea want theirs done like it as well."

Lexie looked pleased. "Ooh, my first commissions! I got the idea when your dad asked if I was a modern day Warhol."

Annie searched around frantically. With everyone milling about, going to the bathroom, and buying concessions, it was hard to spot people. "Have you seen my dad? Is he here?"

Lexie shook her head. "No. Did he say he was coming?"

Annie didn't answer. She waved at Lexie and started backward skating around the track with a few other girls. The buzzer sounded the end of the half-time and Annie skated over to the bench. Coach Ritter sent her out for the second jam but she stopped dead before getting to the blockers' line. Dashing through the door, hair sticking straight up, shirt covered in flour, and wearing his paint-stained trainers, was Dad.

He saw her in the rink and shouted, over the music and loudspeaker, "Go, Beanie!"

Annie blushed then grinned widely. He really was the best dad in the world.

Chapter Seventeen

The two teams were still neck and neck. Every time the Belles racked up some points, the Dolls came around to grab them back, and get some more. Annie's blocking confidence kept getting better and Coach Ritter sent her out as often as the other players on the team.

Ten minutes to the end of the bout things started getting hairy as the tensions got high. The score was 98-96 and both teams wanted desperately to win. Penalties flew as they all started playing more aggressively. During one jam, both teams only had three people on the track: a jammer and two blockers.

Three minutes left and the Belles were only lagging by a few points. Annie hadn't bitten her nails in years but suddenly felt she might restart the habit. Liz, Holly, Cookie, and Natalia were all blocking, Sharmila was jammer. No jammer had made it through the pack yet, though not through lack of trying.

"ElizaDEATH is standing her ground as Polly Socket tries to barge through," Jesse announced. "Sharmila the Hun sees an opening, goes for it, but no! Slam I. Am sends her out of bounds."

Sharmila re-entered the track behind the pack and charged. Liz pushed against the opposing blockers to try and make a gap for Sharmila to slip through. Slam I. Am wasn't having it, though. She shoved back but somehow her legs got in the way, sending Liz flying head over skates. In retaliation, Holly hit Slam illegally with an elbow, and the Derby Doll went crashing to the ground.

A gasp rang through the audience and across the players' bench. Not because of Holly – who was calling Slam a witch and other rude words – but because Liz wasn't getting up. The refs blew a timeout and Coach Ritter rushed over to her captain.

"She practically landed on her head," Lauren said as Annie gripped her friend's arm tightly. If anything happened to Liz…

The crowd clapped supportively as Coach Ritter and one of the refs helped Liz off the track. Carmen cleared a space for Liz on the bench and offered her a water bottle. Liz's eyes were wide and she seemed a bit dazed but kept saying, "I'm OK, I'm OK."

The score was now 84-87 in favour of the Derby Dolls. 2:12 was left on the clock. They'd probably only have time for two more jams, maybe three. Finally convinced that Liz was OK, or would be, Coach Ritter looked at the girls on the bench. Holly was in the box but so was Slam; both teams would start the jam a player short.

Annie fidgeted. She watched Coach Ritter study the girls sitting on the bench. Carmen had her arm around Liz and didn't look like she was willing to let her go. Sharmila and Natalia had skated two jams in a row and looked tired. With Holly in the box, there wasn't anyone else who normally played jammer.

"Annie, you're jammer. Show us that speed."

Annie looked at her coach with wide eyes before standing up and slipping on the helmet panty someone was holding out to her. She couldn't believe it. She was finally getting her chance. Lauren punched her shoulder and followed her out into the rink with Tashi and Bea.

She could hear Holly screaming encouragement from the box. Dad yelled, "That's my Beanie!" Jesse, who was handling the music as well as MC'ing, switched from Def Leppard to The Clash's "London Calling".

The jammer next to her was Mo Jo, and by the scowl on her face she hadn't forgotten how Annie had pushed her out of bounds. Annie would have to break away as soon as that whistle blew to get to the pack before Mo. Just like when they were playing Red Light, Green Light, Annie pushed off with her toe stops the split second she heard the whistle blow. She was at the pack in a heartbeat, frantically looking for that gap to squeeze through. Hell's Angelica looked the other way to help Mo. Annie sucked in her breath and slipped by sideways with the heels of her skates together and toes straight out. Hell's Angelica swivelled round to stop her, but Annie was too fast. The jammer ref blew two rapid whistles and pointed at Annie with his arms in an L-shape.

She was the lead jammer! She could hear the crowd screaming and knew that at least two of those voices belonged to Lexie and Dad. Coming up behind the pack, Mo had just broken through and Annie used the same gap to sneak by herself. Mo looked over her shoulder and at that moment, Annie passed her on the outside.

"Unbelievable, folks. Mo Jo has just been grand slammed by newbie, Anne R. Key!" Jesse called over the loudspeaker.

Annie sprinted around the track, bending down low and leaning into the corners as she flew around. A few crossovers later, the pack loomed ahead of her again. *If I can just get by the other blockers once more, I can call off the jam before Mo scores any more points.*

But from where she was it seemed impossible. The Derby Dolls were determined not to let Annie pass them again. Lauren was trying hard to create a space for Annie to slip through, but so far she hadn't managed to push any of the Derby Dolls out of bounds.

Two strides before getting to the pack Annie had a brilliant idea, "Lauren, leap frog!"

In a flash, Lauren tucked her head and braced herself in a wide snowplough. Annie picked up some extra speed. In her mind, she was at a gymnastics meet going down the runway and Lauren had turned into a vault. There was no springboard, but no matter. Annie wasn't looking for height and multiple turns in mid-air. She just needed to clear the vault, something she'd done since she was eight.

179

Her hands landed square on Lauren's back as she pushed off. Just a basic handspring over the vault. Except as her feet left the ground and she was upside down, Annie remembered this was not gymnastics. The vault was a human, there was no mat beneath her. And she was on skates.

Oh no.

Don't stick the landing, her mind raced. *If I try to stick it, the skates will wipe out from under me and I'll break my bum. Or worse.*

Annie pointed her toes and leaned forward. It was her only hope.

She landed on her toe stops and the momentum dropped her to knees and wrists. Even with the pads that kind of hurt. Kind of, but not enough to stop a derby girl. She got back on her skates in an instant and glided with her arms in the air, her bum out, and back arched. From the bench, Coach Ritter was frantically flapping her arms at her hips.

Oh, right. Annie tapped her hips and called off the jam.

"Dude," Lauren wrapped Annie in a tight hug as they both skated off the rink. "That was insane. *You're* insane!"

"I wouldn't have tried it with anyone but you." Annie hugged Lauren back as she glanced around with shocked wide eyes. *Now that was wicked!*

The rest of the team hugged them both and Coach Ritter shook her head in disbelief. "Please don't do that again. You almost gave me a heart attack."

"Get used to it." Liz put an arm around Annie when she sat on the bench. "Because this year, the Liberty Belles are going to be full of surprises!"

The crowd, though small, were screaming their lungs out. Dad was jumping up and down like a five-year-old on too much sugar. It didn't matter that there were thirty-seven seconds left to the bout. One more jam got played, but no one seemed able to concentrate, let alone score. Not that it mattered. The Liberty Belles were six points ahead when the buzzer sounded to signal the end of the bout.

They did a victory lap around the rink, Liz a bit slower than the rest, and slapped hands with the Derby Dolls and the audience. The Derby Dolls all gave Annie a dirty look as if she had got away with something illegal. But she hadn't. She'd read the whole derby rulebook last week and there was nothing that said she couldn't handspring over the pack.

After the Derby Dolls had done their victory lap, Annie skated over to Dad who was waiting by the side of the rink. Someone, Lexie she guessed, had painted "Anne R. Key" across his forehead like football fans did at home. Annie's smile spread from ear to ear. One of the best days of her life, for sure.

Dad lifted Annie off her skates in a big hug. "Wow, Beanie. That was amazing. Next time I tell you to be a cheerleader instead, just ignore me. Really. Or tell me to shut up."

Annie buried her head in his shoulder. "I was afraid you weren't going to make it."

"Miss out on something this important to you? Never!" he said before kissing her forehead and putting her down.

"You should be proud." Coach Ritter came up and shook

Dad's hand. "I've never seen anything like that before. Or a newbie advance so quickly."

Dad's hand ran through his hair which made it lie flat for once instead of sticking straight up. He tried to brush off the flour from his shirt but had no luck there. "Annie's always been very determined. When she's good at something she won't stop until she's risen to the top."

"Does she get that from you?"

"Good god, no. That's all from her mother. My ex," Dad added quickly as his face turned pink.

Annie cringed a bit at Dad's comment. "Ex" sounded so final. There was still a chance her parents might get back together, right? She didn't have time to think about that as Lexie came over and gave her a big hug.

"That was the best thing ever! You couldn't have done that as a cheerleader," Lexie said.

Annie grinned the huge smile she hadn't been able to muster during the cheerleading try-outs.

"This is loads better than cheerleading. For one thing, the music rocks," Annie called to Jesse who was busy putting away the sound system.

"You got that right." He blew the hair out of his gorgeous eyes and flashed her a brilliant smile. "You've got to show me how to do the handspring thing on wheels. That was sweet!"

"You're on!"

Annie turned back to Lexie, Dad, and Coach Ritter. Dad put his arm around Annie's shoulders, giving them a squeeze.

"If you ever want to become an NSO – non-skating official," Coach Ritter was saying to Dad, "we can always use some extra hands."

Dad nodded, glancing at one of the NSOs in pirate gear wiping clean the penalty board. "That could be fun. Can't let Annie have all the glory."

Annie gave her dad a gentle shove. "You just want to wear a funky outfit."

"I get to wear a funky outfit? Dude!" Dad bobbed his head with a cheesy grin. Annie rolled her eyes. Dad was a nutter. But she wouldn't trade him for any other.

Lexie, sensing Annie's embarrassment, turned to her. "I'm starving. You guys have any food?"

Dad's head snapped to attention at the sound of his favourite word. "Good thinking. All right, Liberty Belles, back to Rosie Lee's for the after-party."

There was a cheer from the remaining Belles on the rink and they went to tell the girls already getting changed in the locker room. Dad smiled to himself and turned back to Coach Ritter. "Will you come too, Susan?"

Coach Ritter blushed slightly. "Sorry. I have to pick up my kids. From their father's."

"Ah, well maybe next time." Dad shook the coach's hand. Did he hold onto it just a smidgen longer than necessary? Nah, she was just imagining things. Annie pushed the thought out of her head as she skated to the locker room.

"Hey, Anne R. Key," a college-aged girl called out. "You were awesome out there. Can't wait to see what else you can do."

"Cheers." Annie waved before going into the locker room. She couldn't wait to see what would happen either. What a great day. Annie had proven she could be good at something other than gymnastics. She couldn't wait to tell Mum.

Chapter Eighteen

Back at Rosie Lee's, Dad set out a huge plate of the Earl Grey cupcakes Annie and Lexie had invented along with spiced cookies and chocolate peanut butter brownies. Most of the team had made it, including Lexie, who was definitely an honorary team member. Sadly, Jesse had to work at the rink, so their other honorary member wasn't there.

"I still can't believe you, Annie," Lauren said as she helped herself to another brownie.

"I hope someone caught that on video," Carmen said.

Sharmila picked at the cookie crumbs left on her plate. "I'm sure my baba did. He videos everything any of us does."

"Where did you learn to do that?" Tashi asked.

Annie didn't know what to say. At that moment it had seemed

like the most logical way to get past the pack. Now just the thought that she had done a handspring on skates, over a human, made her wonder if she should get her sanity examined. Still, she couldn't change how amazing it had felt.

"Let's just say, I was really, really lucky to pull that off." Annie grinned as she licked the icing off her cupcake. Annie knew that if she'd touched any other player while her feet were air in the air, the daring move would have got her a major penalty.

"Well, we're really lucky to have all of you on the team," Liz said, determined not to play favourites.

"Watch out, Holly, Annie just might take your place as the team's best jammer," Sharmila said as she hid her face behind a mug of sweet tea.

Holly stuck her tongue out at Sharmila good-naturedly but Annie had the feeling the comment stung more than she was willing to admit. "Just you wait," Holly retorted. "I'll do a double axel over the pack one of these days. You guys don't need your heads, right?"

The team booed at Holly who laughed and playfully threw her napkin at them.

Liz raised her glass of the "champagne" Dad had mixed up: white grape juice and fizzy water. "Here's to the best team Liberty Belles has ever had. We couldn't have won today without *any* of you."

"Here, here!" They all cheered and laughed. Annie couldn't help grinning. It had been a long time since she'd been part of a crowd that really made her feel like she belonged. She doubted the cheerleading squad would have been as welcoming, not with Kelsey as queen bee.

"Ooh, check it. The whole soccer team is walking by." Sharmila pointed out of the window.

Annie jerked around so quickly, she knocked over her glass. Thankfully it was empty and it didn't break. Sure enough, there was Tyler walking by the café with some of his teammates. He looked like he'd just got out of the shower, comb marks still visible in his wet hair. Annie wanted nothing more than to mess it up.

Of course. There had been a game tonight. By the cheers the roller girls could hear from outside the café, the soccer team must have won. There were some girls laughing and hanging out with them too. Cheerleaders mostly, Annie recognized them. Including Kelsey.

Not that it mattered. Tyler turned at that very moment. His green eyes landed on her brown ones and he burst into a huge smile.

"Yo, Ann-nie!" He held out a hand and waved from the other side of the glass.

Everyone – roller girls, soccer players, and cheerleaders – turned to stare at Annie. Any other time she would have ducked under the table and not come out until she was twenty. But not tonight. Tonight she had vaulted over the pack and helped win the game for her team. Tonight was her night.

She waved back and even though her cheeks were a bit pink, she sent him a smile that matched his.

The cheerleaders gave Annie a dirty look as the soccer team

hooted and dragged Tyler away. Before they turned the corner, Tyler looked over his shoulder and waved one last time.

Annie's teammates, who had been watching the exchange in silence, burst into wild giggling. Dad poked his head out of the kitchen with a blob of dough in his hands before rolling his eyes and retreating back to the safety of knives and hot ovens.

"Yo, Ann-nie," Sharmila imitated Tyler's tone exactly. "Will you marry me?"

"Dang, girl. He's only the hottest guy in school," Carmen teased.

A few other girls started making kissing noises.

Annie blushed more now than she had when Tyler had called her name loud enough for the whole street to hear. "Oh, shut it."

"Whatever, you love it." Holly flicked some of her crumbs in Annie's direction.

Annie swatted them away and grinned sheepishly. "Yeah, I kind of do."

"You're so lucky. I'd give anything to go out with him," Cookie sighed.

Annie saw her moment. Even though Cookie seemed to think it was a done deal, Annie had to know for sure. "Isn't he going out with anyone, then?"

"Who would?" Lexie mumbled.

"Not me." Lauren folded her arms over her chest.

Annie narrowed her eyes. Of course Lexie would say that, she hated jocks, but Lauren grew up in a family of jocks. Annie brushed it away. That wasn't important right now. Not when

Carmen answered her question.

"Tyler broke up with his girlfriend over the summer." Carmen looked at Annie with a smirk. "Looks like you've got a chance."

The girls cheered and continued to tease Annie. Who cared? She had a chance with Tyler. A few weeks ago, she would have never thought it was possible.

I love it here!

Dad put the kettle on when they got home while Annie rushed to the computer to see if there was any chance Mum might still be awake. The Skype icon said she was and Annie called her right away.

"Aw, Mum, you should have been there, it was brilliant. It was the first time they played me as jammer. There was no way around or through so I had to go over with a handspring. You should have seen the looks on the other team's faces when I flew over them."

Mum pushed up her glasses and frowned as she stared intently at the screen. "What do you mean you did a handspring over some girl's back? Didn't you tell me roller derby is played on skates?"

"Yeah—" Annie started but she was cut off.

"That sounds very dangerous, sweetheart. You shouldn't take such risks."

Annie sighed. Doing front tucks on the balance beam

had been OK but vaulting on skates was dangerous. "It was fine. Really."

Mum shook her head. "I worry about you. If something happened to you being so far away, I... Why don't you come back? It would be so nice having you here again. Your room is just how you left it."

Annie looked around Aunt Julie's old room. She had finally started to make it look more like a modern teenager's room with posters of her favourite bands, some artwork by Lexie, and the team photo of the Illinoisies she had printed off the internet. On the bedside table was a picture of Dad, Mum, and herself laughing. It had been a great day, but it was a few years old; Annie must have been around ten. Realistically, she knew her parents probably wouldn't get back together. "I've had my ups and downs, I know, but I'm really starting to fit in. Besides, I'm not a quitter, Mum. I got that from you."

Mum smiled a mixture of pride and sadness. "I guess I did something right, then. Well, I'm off to bed."

"Night, Mum." Annie moved the mouse to end the call when Mum spoke up again.

"Oh, Annie?"

"Yeah?"

"That room is a mess. Please pick up those clothes I see on the floor."

Annie rolled her eyes and laughed. "Love you, Mum."

"Love you too."

Annie sat by the computer for a couple of seconds, looking

around the room some more. She wasn't just saying it. She did like it here. Very much. With a smile, she threw her clothes into a pile in the corner and went to the living room. She found Dad waiting for her with a cuppa.

"I liked your teammates. They're a good bunch."

Annie let the steam rise over her face as she breathed deeply. Dad had broken down and bought good quality tea for the house. "I like them too."

Dad's eyes glowed as he mimed Annie's handspring with his hands. "And you were so amazing out there. Now I can see why you like roller derby so much. I'm really proud of you."

Annie set down her tea and smiled at him. "I'm proud of you too, Dad. I mean look at Rosie Lee's. It's your dream and it's come true."

"Indeed, indeed." Dad stretched out on the couch and closed his eyes. For a second, Annie thought he'd fallen asleep, until he said, "Yup, I do think this derby thing is not that bad after all."

Annie couldn't resist the opportunity to tease Dad. "Does your change of heart have anything to do with how pretty Coach Ritter is?"

Dad opened his eyes and feigned innocence. "I didn't even notice."

"You were totally checking her out," Annie teased.

Dad sat up, his cheeks a rosy pink. He so rarely got embarrassed that Annie realized she was right. "Listen to you sounding all American."

Now it was Annie's turn to blush. She hadn't intended to

sound American, it just came out that way. Still, she could work with that for now. "Shucks. Sure looks like it, partner. Might jus' have to stick round these here parts, keep you in line."

Dad laughed and clinked his mug against hers. "We make a good team, String Bean, don't we?"

"The best!"

ALL ABOUT Roller Derby

RULES OF THE GAME

A roller derby game is called a bout. A bout usually lasts sixty minutes and is divided into two-minute jams. During a jam, each of the two teams have five players on the track, all skating in the same direction. The blockers and pivots form a tight pack. The two jammers start behind them and race to break through the pack. The first jammer through the pack is designated the lead jammer. However, no points can be scored until the jammer passes the pack for a second time. The jammer then scores a point for every opponent that she overtakes, provided she passes the player in bounds and without penalties. Both jammers may score points for the duration of the two-minute jam or until the lead jammer calls off the jam. A jammer typically scores four points every time she makes it through the pack. If she overtakes the other jammer she scores a fifth point, and this is known as a Grand Slam. The team with the most points at the end of the bout wins.

PIVOTS

BLOCKERS

JAMMERS

REFEREES

JAMMER REFEREES

SKATER POSITIONS

 JAMMER
The jammer wears a helmet cover with a star and is the
only player who can score points. To score points, a jammer
must break through the pack once and sprint around the
track. A jammer scores a point for every opponent she
passes on her subsequent passes through the pack.

LEAD JAMMER
The lead jammer is the first jammer to break through the
pack and pass all the opposing blockers and pivot. The lead
jammer may choose, at a strategic time, to call off the jam
to prevent the opposing jammer from scoring. She does this
by putting her hands on her hips.

 PIVOT
The pivot acts as a pacesetter for the team and is designated
by a striped helmet. The pivot calls out plays and provides
guidance for the rest of the team. The pivot typically stays
in front of the blockers.

 BLOCKER
Each team has three blockers on the track. The blockers
play both offensive and defensive roles. They help their
jammer get through the pack, while trying to prevent the
opposing jammer from getting through.

PENALTIES

There are many rules in the sport of roller derby, enforced by referees and non-skating officials (NSOs). If a skater commits a major penalty, she is sent to the penalty box, also known as the sin bin, for sixty seconds. If a jammer is sent to the penalty box, the opposing team's jammer scores a point for the missing player if she passes through the pack. If both jammers are sent to the penalty box, the first jammer is released as soon as the second jammer reaches the box.

OFFENCES RESULTING IN A MAJOR PENALTY INCLUDE:

- ☒ Tripping an opposing player
- ☒ Back blocking
- ☒ Using elbows to the chest or face
- ☒ Swearing at another skater or referee
- ☒ Blocking twenty feet ahead or behind the pack
- ☒ Deliberately falling in front of another player
- ☒ Grabbing, pulling or pushing an opposing player

HISTORY OF ROLLER DERBY

Roller derby was first played in the 1930s and quickly evolved into a popular spectator sport, thanks to staged crashes and collisions. By 1940 it was watched by about five million spectators, but by the 1970s the sport had faded into obscurity. At the beginning of the twenty-first century, a roller derby revival began in Austin, Texas and soon spread to many other cities and countries. Modern roller derby has focused on athleticism rather than showmanship. It is the fastest-growing sport in America, and is under consideration to become an Olympic sport at the 2020 games!

Read on for a sneak peek at the next
Roller Girls book...

Hell's Belles

$3x - 7 = 2x - 2$ Solve for x.

Annie sighed. She had no idea how to solve for x, but there was a lemon tart in the display case that would help solve the growling in her stomach.

She swept her long brown hair into a messy bun, closed her maths book and thought up her own equation: Annie + a steaming cup of chamomile tea = heaven.

Pushing aside her homework, she rose and crossed the black and white checkerboard floor of Rosie Lee's, the café she and her dad had recently opened in his hometown of Liberty Heights, Illinois. It was hard to believe that a few short weeks ago, the shop had been filthy and covered in cobwebs. A lot of hard work had gone into transforming it into the cosy place it was now, but it had been a labour of love – the shop was Dad's dream.

Although from the frown on his face as he bent over the spreadsheets arranged on the counter, the dream looked like it had become a nightmare. Annie guessed that he was having some maths trouble too.

"I must take after you," Annie joked, reaching into the case and removing the cream-topped pastry. "No head for numbers."

"You can say that again," Dad grumbled. He dropped his pencil and ran a hand through his brown hair. "I can measure out baking powder with the best of them and calculate the proportion of butter to flour with my eyes closed. It's subtracting monthly expenses from income that trips me up."

Annie glanced around the empty shop and grimaced. Things had got off to a good start, but lately the only foot traffic in and out of the shop consisted of people popping in to hang notices on the "community bulletin board" Dad had installed. The people had been grateful for the advertising space, but once they'd pinned their flyers to the corkboard, they'd hurried off to finish distributing their materials. The guy who'd posted an index card advertising a "2003 Toyota Camry with low mileage" had bought himself a small coffee to go, but other than that, none of the bulletin board people had purchased a thing.

"So has there been any?" Annie asked. "Income, I mean."

Dad hesitated, as though he might be about to fib. Then he showed her the number on the calculator screen. "Not much, Beanie."

Annie rolled her eyes at the use of his nickname for her.

Beanie was short for "String Bean", which referred to Annie's long, lanky frame. She'd shot up nearly a foot last year which had sadly put a swift end to her gymnastics career. On the upside, she now had the tall, slender figure of a model. She really didn't mind the Beanie thing. It was so Dad – cute and a little bit silly.

What wasn't silly was the money issue. Nothing cute about "not much income". Annie had been afraid that would be the case. When they'd opened the British eatery they'd both had high hopes. Dad's baking was superior and the space was warm and welcoming. It had seemed like a no-brainer to Annie – they were going to be a big hit. But here it was, four weeks later on a crisp, early autumn afternoon; customers should have been flocking in for hot tea and cinnamon scones warm from the oven. Instead, the cheery little place was utterly deserted.

As though he were reading her mind, Dad motioned to the empty tables. "I must be doing something wrong, but for the life of me, Annie, I can't imagine what it is."

His voice was a mixture of confusion and disappointment. It made Annie's heart sink.

"Don't say that, Dad," she said, placing the tart on the counter and throwing her arms around him. "You're doing everything right. The food is brilliant, the shop is the cutest place in town, and … and…" Unfortunately, she didn't have a third "and" to add, so she just hugged him tighter. "It'll be fine. It takes time for a place like Rosie Lee's to catch on. But once it does, we'll have customers queuing round the block."

Dad pressed a kiss to Annie's forehead and chuckled. "Now

I remember why I dragged you here all the way from London. To be my own personal cheerleader."

Annie winced. Sore subject. She'd been chosen for the Liberty Heights High School cheerleading squad, but had had the audacity to turn them down. That decision had pretty much made her Public Enemy Number One in the eyes of Kelsey Howard, the most popular girl in school. Instead of picking up a pair of pom-poms, she'd stepped into a pair of roller skates and joined Liberty Heights' junior roller derby league.

And derby girls, it seemed, were always hungry.

Tummy grumbling, she picked up the lemon tart, then pointed to a gorgeous chocolate-frosted cake under a glass dome on top of the display case.

"Gather your rations, sailor," she commanded, doing her best Navy Admiral impersonation. "Then muster at our usual table."

"Aye, aye, captain," said Dad, snapping her a silly salute. He punched the off button on his calculator and grabbed a knife.

Moments later they were seated by the large window, bent over their desserts. Annie tasted Dad's cake – it was beyond delicious. And the buttery crust of her lemon tart was so delicate that it actually melted in her mouth. If only people would try Rosie Lee's, she was certain it would become their favourite place in the world.

"You really outdid yourself with this batch," she told her father, using her baby finger to mop up a smear of lemon filling from her plate. "Who cares if you're hopeless with numbers and spreadsheets. You're an absolute wizard in the kitchen."

Dad gave her a grateful smile. "I appreciate the rave review, Beanie, but the fact remains: we need customers if we're going to stay afloat." He put down his fork and stared at the mural on the wall behind Annie. It was a red double-decker London bus filled with remarkably lifelike portraits of some of Britain's most celebrated citizens. And the best part was that it was custom-designed and hand-painted by Annie's best friend, Lexie.

But Annie could see from the look on Dad's face that he was suddenly missing one British citizen in particular. "If your mum were here she'd certainly get our financials in order," he said softly.

"Maybe." Annie frowned. "But she's *not* here."

After her parents separated, Annie's American-born Dad had decided to leave England and return to the United States. Annie had been given the choice to remain in London with Mum, or try life in America with Dad. It had been the most difficult decision of her life, but ultimately she'd chosen to go with Dad. Throughout Annie's whole life, it was always Dad who had really been there for her. Mum loved Annie and Annie loved her, but she was always busy at her law firm.

The truth was, Annie missed her mother a lot, but this wasn't the time to wallow in that. Dad needed to get his confidence back and thinking about his failed marriage and his ex-wife, thousands of miles away across the ocean, probably wasn't the way to do it.

On the other hand, Annie felt a little tingle of hope. If Dad missed Mum – and maybe not just for her business skills – that could mean there was a chance they'd consider trying again. Of course, that would require Mum taking her nose out of her law books and legal briefs long enough to miss him, too.

Dad was still looking wistfully at the mural. "It was a gamble, taking you away from all your friends and bringing you to America. I hope I didn't make a mistake."

"You didn't," Annie assured him. "Going to an American high school is amazing. It's like being in a teen drama! Honestly, sometimes I think I'm going to walk into the cafeteria and see the cast of *Glee* or *90210*. It's been really fun."

"Good – as long as you don't turn into a drama queen yourself!" Dad joked.

Annie had enough real-life, Liberty Heights High drama queens to deal with already. But she didn't mention that to her father.

"And you didn't *take* me," she reminded him, slapping her hand on the white tablecloth. "I chose to come. And here I am. So let's not be gloomy about it. Let's figure out a way to make it work!"

Dad sat back in the chair and blinked at her. Annie knew he was surprised by her assertiveness. Frankly, so was she. The old Annie had been more quiet and reserved, and a lot less confident. The old Annie might have turned and ran the minute the cheerleader captain, Kelsey, looked at her sideways. The old Annie probably would have already accepted defeat and begun packing her bags to head back across the ocean to London.

But the old Annie wasn't a roller girl!

Annie popped up from her chair and put one hand on her hip,

affecting the persona of a cranky, wise-cracking diner waitress.

"You done here, pal? We got other customers waitin' for this table, ya know. Meatloaf's the blue plate special tonight. Can't keep them regulars away when that one's on the menu." She chomped on her imaginary chewing gum. "So you ready to pay, or what?"

Dad faked a frown. "Well, since I know the chef personally, I thought this might be on the house."

"Oh, fine." Annie rolled her eyes and pretended to fluff her imaginary beehive hairdo. "Just be sure you leave a decent tip. You think I woik my tail off in this joint for the fun of it?"

Dad quickly reached into his pocket and pulled out a couple of notes.

"Jeesh," she huffed, sweeping up the bills from the tabletop and tucking them into the neckline of her shirt. "Two whole bucks. Ain't that generous? I'll try not to spend it all in one place!"

With a clatter, she gathered the plates and cutlery from the table, balanced them on her palm and held them high above her head as she sashayed off towards the kitchen. She could hear Dad's laughter following her all the way to the sink.

Annie was pleased at having made Dad laugh. He needed some distraction from all the pressure. As she ran hot water over the chocolate smudges on the plate and brushed the crumbs of tart crust into the drain, she thought about the two dollars Dad had "tipped" her. It gave her an idea.

Why couldn't she *really* bring in a little extra money? She was fourteen years old, after all. She should be contributing. And not just by working for free at Rosie Lee's – by actually earning some extra cash.

So what could she do? Between school, homework, and her roller derby practice schedule, she'd need extremely flexible hours. And she knew that here, anyone under sixteen wasn't allowed to work at night during the school year. This was going to take some serious thought.

She dried her hands on a paper towel and returned to the cosy little dining area where Dad had gone back to his invoices and bank statements. He was attacking his paperwork with new resolve and she didn't want to bother him. So she went back to the table where she'd left her algebra homework and sat down.

But she couldn't concentrate on her assignment.

She had to find a way to earn some extra money until the shop got off the ground...

Read *Hell's Belles* to find out what Annie does next!

Hooked on roller derby?

Here are three more fast and furious *Roller Girls* books about Annie and her friends.

Hell's Belles

Annie Turner's roller derby team, the Liberty Belles, is finally on a winning streak. Full of confidence, the girls plan a Halloween bout with the High Rollers, their tough and cheeky arch-rivals. There'll be costumes, gruesome make-up and plenty of trash talk to look forward to. But when Annie's crush asks her to a Halloween dance on the same night, she finds herself torn between her girls and her man.

Will Annie's first American Halloween turn out to be more 'trick' than 'treat'?

In a Jam

Life couldn't be better for Annie Turner. Not only is she going out with the dreamiest boy she's ever met, but her roller derby team is riding high in the league. But OF COURSE, just when things seem to be working out, it all starts falling apart. Annie gets left on the bench at a big bout, her best friend can't stand her boyfriend and her mum wants her to quit the team!

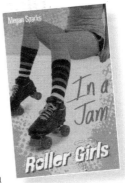

Will Annie listen to her heart? And what is it saying, anyway?

Boot Camp Blues

Annie Turner is single again and it really kind of sucks. It doesn't help that her ex is now going out with a cheerleader! But she's also confused by her new feelings for skater boy Jesse. They're just friends … aren't they? Meanwhile, Annie and her roller girls are each desperate to make the cut for an all-star team. Tensions run high as the teammates compete against each other for roller glory.

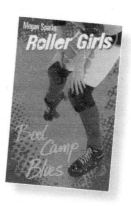

Will the stars in Annie's eyes get in the way of her friendships?

For more exciting books from brilliant
authors, follow the fox!
www.curious-fox.com